PUFFIN BOOKS

GRANDPARENTS' BAG OF STORIES

Sudha Murty was born in 1950 in Shiggaon, north Karnataka. She did her MTech in computer science and is now the chairperson of the Infosys Foundation. A prolific writer in English and Kannada, she has written novels, technical books, travelogues, collections of short stories and non-fictional pieces and several bestselling titles for children. Her books have been translated into all the major Indian languages. Sudha Murty is the recipient of the R.K. Narayan Award for Literature (2006), the Padma Shri (2006), the Attimabbe Award from the Government of Karnataka for excellence in Kannada literature (2011) and most recently, the Lifetime Achievement Award at the 2018 Crossword Book Awards.

Also in Puffin by Sudha Murty

SUDHA MURTY

GRANDPARENTS'
Bag *of* Stories

Illustrations by Priya Kuriyan

PUFFIN BOOKS
An imprint of Penguin Random House

PUFFIN BOOKS

USA | Canada | UK | Ireland | Australia
New Zealand | India | South Africa | China

Puffin Books is part of the Penguin Random House group of companies
whose addresses can be found at global.penguinrandomhouse.com

Published by Penguin Random House India Pvt. Ltd
4th Floor, Capital Tower 1, MG Road,
Gurugram 122 002, Haryana, India

Penguin
Random House
India

First published in Puffin Books by Penguin Random House India 2020

Text copyright © Sudha Murty 2020
Illustrations copyright © Priya Kuriyan 2020

All rights reserved

17 16

This is a work of fiction. Names, characters, places and incidents are either the
product of the author's imagination or are used fictitiously and any resemblance
to any actual person, living or dead, events or locales is entirely coincidental.

ISBN 9780143451846

Typeset in Cochin by Manipal Technologies Limited, Manipal
Printed at Thomson Press India Ltd, New Delhi

www.penguin.co.in

MIX
Paper
FSC FSC® C010615

To Kaka,
and to the medical fraternity
who continue to fight every day to keep us safe

Contents

Contents

Preface

As I began to get used to working from home during the time of coronavirus, I looked for entertaining ways to spend the limited extra time I found on my hands. To get away from the news and heavy discussions related to the virus, I began doing what I do best—create stories.

My imagination ran wild and free and the stories seemed to flow seamlessly, almost as if this book was meant to be written. I became both Ajji and Ajja, the main characters of the book, and some days, I felt like the children in the book too! The days went by quickly. Even as the book revealed itself, I learnt the importance of having a routine, being positive, accepting the new normal and working towards the goal of helping people less fortunate than me.

Sunanda, my sister, is a doctor, as was my father Dr R.H. Kulkarni, also popularly known as Kaka. Through their work, I observed their dedication to patients and without even knowing it, in my younger days, I developed compassion towards people going through medical challenges. Today, doctors, nurses and housekeeping workers are putting their lives on the line more than ever before, to fight against the virus and protect our country. That is the reason this book is dedicated to them.

A heartfelt thanks to Shrutkeerti Khurana, my friend and trusted editor, whose passion made the journey of this book a cheerful one, despite the lockdown.

Lastly, this book would not have been possible without you, my little readers. You are the inspiration that keeps me going.

The Arrival of Rice
and the Children

It was a pleasant afternoon in March. Ajji and Ajja were glued to the television. The worry on their faces deepened as they heard increasingly distressing news about the coronavirus situation. Ajja turned to Ajji, 'The virus started in China, but look at what has happened. It has spread all over the world, becoming a pandemic!'

The anchor on the television announced, 'The government is asking people to isolate themselves and follow social distancing protocols. All schools will be closed until further notice.'

Ajji's thoughts turned to her grandchildren in Bangalore and Mumbai.

The sound of an autorickshaw coming to a stop outside the house interrupted her thoughts and the bell rang.

Ding-dong!

Ajji opened the door and saw Kamlu, Ajja's sister, and her granddaughter Aditi. Ajji was delighted and surprised to see them. 'Come inside,' she said.

Kamlu Ajji smiled as she took the bags out of the autorickshaw.

'Why didn't you tell us you were coming?' asked Ajji. 'We would have picked you up from the railway station.

Kamlu Ajji and Aditi entered the house.

'Kamlu, why did you make this trip with the deadly virus around?' Ajja demanded, concerned.

'Oh, I didn't know coronavirus had reached here too. Isn't it time for the cart festival now? I haven't seen it in so long! Aditi has her holidays now and her mother is working from home, so it is hard to keep her engaged. I thought she might enjoy the festival and brought her with me. Besides, I wanted to give you a surprise!'

Nine-year-old Aditi stood shyly behind Kamlu Ajji. 'Come, child. Sit,' said Ajji, inviting her with love.

They all went to sit in the living room, and just then, the phone rang.

Ajji picked it up. It was her daughter, Sumati, from Mumbai. 'Amma,' she said, 'I am sending both the kids to you in Shiggaon.'

'I'd be happy to have Raghu and Meenu, but what happened?'

'With Covid-19 spreading like wildfire, the schools are closing down for some time and no one knows when they will reopen. Most people live in small apartments in Mumbai and it is almost impossible to keep children from going outside. Moreover, we are working from home and can't tend to their needs all the time. So we thought about it and spoke to Subhadra to see if I could send Raghu and Meenu to her, and she said yes . . .'

'All the children can come here, Sumati!' Ajji interrupted her.

'I knew you would say that and that's why I called. Subhadra has also agreed to send her children to Shiggaon to be with you. You have a large compound around the house and there's plenty of fresh air and space to move around. This way, the kids can be with you all and not get bored since they will be able to play with each other. Now, don't hesitate to be frank. Tell me, will it be a problem for you to handle the four of them without sending them outside the house?'

'No, Sumati, that is not a problem at all! My worry is — how will they come here?'

'We will take care of that, Amma! Raghu and Meenu have already taken a flight from Mumbai to Bangalore today and are about to reach Subhadra's home,' said Sumati. 'They can come to Shiggaon tomorrow and stay for a few weeks.'

Ajja, who had been listening to Ajji's side of the call, took the phone from her and spoke to Sumati, 'Don't worry, child. Kamlu and her granddaughter Aditi are also here. Send the children.'

Almost immediately, there was another call from Bangalore. Subhadra was on the line. She said the same thing. 'My parents have already taken Anand with them, but Krishna and Anoushka want to see you and stay in Shiggaon. I have spoken to Sumati already and the four children will reach your home tomorrow. Our office manager has offered to drive them from Bangalore to Shiggaon, but he will come back immediately because there is a lot of work to be taken care of before things get worse, as is expected,' said Subhadra.

Ajji ended the call and looked at Ajja. 'I am happy to hear that our grandchildren are coming, but I am concerned about the coronavirus situation. Will you call the temple and check if the cart festival is still going ahead as planned?'

Ajja nodded and dialled the temple's number. While calling, he remarked, 'It is unlikely that they'll go ahead with the festival. We had a committee meeting yesterday and I suggested that we skip the cart festival this year, but others rejected my opinion. They felt that we shouldn't worry because the coronavirus hasn't reached us yet. I disagreed. Conducting the festival will be akin to giving coronavirus an invitation to come here.'

Kamlu Ajji's face fell. 'Instead of surprising you, I am the one who is surprised and disappointed. I think I will go back after a few days.'

Kamlu Ajji and Ajji were close friends. Ajji was pleased that her friend was with her. 'You are not going anywhere,' she said emphatically. 'Cart festival or not, you are staying here with us.'

Ajja turned out to be right. The festival had been cancelled.

Kamlu Ajji turned to Ajji and announced, 'I am going to take charge of your kitchen. I love cooking. You can rest for a few days.'

Ajja added, 'If the situation with respect to the coronavirus gets worse and a lockdown is announced, then we should not bring any outside help for the work around the house. Let's share the work.'

'Yes, I agree. We can't call anyone,' said Ajji. 'Once the children arrive tomorrow, I will assign household chores to all of them. They will also help us.'

Ajji went to the storeroom to check if she needed to get more groceries. Ajja followed her and remarked, 'Some places have already announced lockdowns. If we have a lockdown here too, there will be many people who will not get enough food. We must help and lend a hand when the time comes. Please order extra rations and keep them in the storeroom. We may need them to feed other people.'

Ajji began to make a grocery list, and Ajja dialled the number of the local grocery shop for a home delivery.

Meanwhile, Aditi sat nearby, reading a book. She was happy to hear that four of her cousins were coming.

The next evening, Raghu, Meenu, Krishna and Anoushka arrived with great excitement. They loved visiting their grandparents' large and spacious home where they were pampered and allowed their freedom.

The office manager dropped the kids and promptly left.

As soon as they entered the house, Aditi squealed and joined them immediately. Anoushka had grown tall. Ajji announced, 'Anoushka, you are the tallest of the girls now!'

The children had brought their schoolbooks, and many bottles of sanitizer and handwash refill packs. They seemed happy to be away from their parents with no classes or teachers to worry about. They told their grandparents how sanitizers were being used everywhere in their schools before they had closed and in their apartment blocks in Mumbai and Bangalore, including even the lift.

'Have things become that difficult there?' Ajji asked, concerned.

'Yes,' said Raghu. 'The government is taking many precautions and has become quite strict.'

'Children, what would you like to eat for dinner?'

'Something light, Ajji, as we had heavy snacks a short time ago,' said Krishna.

'Then I'll make some special rice today—perhaps methi rice,' said Kamlu Ajji. 'It is easy to digest, delicious and good for supper.'

The children agreed and Kamlu Ajji headed to the kitchen.

Ajja switched on the television. Discussions about quarantine and social isolation continued on all news channels. The prime minister was going to address the nation shortly. Ajja looked outside the window. The evening was turning into night. He sighed, 'Children, this is serious now and we all must stay inside the walls of the house. You can only go as far as the wall of the compound. We must not go out for any reason.'

In less than an hour, Kamlu Ajji had made an excellent dish of methi rice with cucumber raita.

Proudly, Ajja said, 'All these vegetables are from our vegetable garden. We use natural fertilizers and grow organic vegetables that taste much better than what you get outside.'

After dinner, the children helped Ajji in laying down five mattresses next to each other. Each of them chose the bed they wanted. Once it was done, Raghu turned to Ajji, 'You have not completed your daily routine.'

Ajji smiled. She knew what he was referring to. 'A story, Ajji,' pleaded Anoushka. 'A story a day keeps all difficulties away . . .'

Everyone chuckled.

'Okay, I will tell you a story. It is a tale of what you ate for dinner—about rice. Rice is part of our daily diet and we can't imagine living without rice or wheat today.'

The children gathered around both the Ajjis.

Ajja sat on a chair nearby, watching the television. The prime minister announced, 'A lockdown will be imposed starting midnight. Everyone must stay home for the next few weeks.'

It was evening and already dark outside. The children began listening to the story earnestly, just as the quarantine period was formally declared. Ajja muted the volume on the television, but continued watching.

'Let us all listen to the story of how rice came to earth,' said Ajji.

A long time ago, humans could walk on clouds and wander freely in heaven.

One day, Madhav, a mortal, became curious about how gods lived in heaven. *Where do they work? What do they do all day? What do they eat?* he wondered.

So, he walked up to heaven and met many gods. He found that there were several gods and goddesses responsible for different departments in the realm.

There was the god of water, the goddess of learning, the god of courage, and the god of good health, among others. But the goddess of grains, Annapurna, fascinated Madhav the most.

He asked her, 'Devi, I want to see the way the agriculture system works here. What do you eat, and how do you produce it?'

Annapurna called him home and fed him a sumptuous meal. One of the ingredients was a delicious soft, white food that looked like a grain. 'I have never seen or eaten this before! I don't think anyone on earth has, either. It is delectable. What is this?' he asked.

'This is rice. All gods eat rice. It gives us energy and mixes very well with all vegetables.'

Madhav agreed with her. 'As long as I am here, I would love to eat this every day,' he said earnestly.

The goddess smiled. 'Of course, Madhav! Eat as much as your heart desires.'

The next day, Madhav asked her, 'How is rice grown here? Will you please show me?'

Since he was really keen to know, Annapurna took him to the rice fields to show how the bed was prepared, how the seeds were sown, how the water was retained and how it was replanted during the different stages of its growth. When the rice grains were ready for harvest, they took on a golden colour and formed a bunch. *Such a beautiful sight to look at*, he thought.

After that, the goddess showed him how the harvest was pounded from grain to rice. There were a variety of pounding styles and each style had a different name. Rice emerged from the pounded grain, which was then ready to cook for a meal.

Madhav spent a few more days in heaven and then asked for the goddess's permission to go back to earth. During his last dinner there, he thought of his wife, his parents, his children, his siblings and his village,

'I want everyone to taste the magic of rice at least once in their lifetimes, even if it is just one teaspoon. I am afraid to ask the goddess, she is sure to refuse my request since this is the food of the gods after all.'

So Madhav took four seeds of rice and hid them in his turban. He knew no one would think of looking for the seeds there.

Madhav came back to earth, quickly planted the seeds and took care of them the same way Annapurna had shown him. When it was time for harvest, he followed the process; he pounded and made the rice. He made a sweet rice dish with the white rice, then closed his eyes and first offered it to the goddess of grains.

Annapurna heard his prayers in heaven and came down to earth*.

When she saw the rice, she became furious. She said, 'Madhav, you have betrayed my trust. I respect the love for knowledge and appreciate your curiosity, but you have stolen from me. Had you been truthful, I would have given you some myself. You must be punished for being a thief.'

Madhav touched her feet and apologized, 'Mother, I did this because of my insecurity. Please forgive me. We are all your children, and I wanted to share

13

the taste of rice with others too. It was not just for my selfishness. Moreover, I have also shared the knowledge of growing rice with others. This is so much better than what we eat and it makes us energetic too. Wouldn't you like your children to have this? Please, I request you to pardon me.'

Annapurna sighed, 'I can't argue with that. I know that your intentions were good. Now that rice is here on earth too, I will always send a sign when it is the right time to sow seeds. I will wash my hair in heaven, and when I push my head back, the wet hair will fall on my back and the water will flow down as rain to the earth. That will be the best time for humans to sow the seeds. The only punishment that I can give now is that no mortal will be allowed to come freely to heaven any more. They will be allowed to do so only after they discard their body at death.'

This is how rice started growing on earth.

*Even today, people who grow rice offer the first produce (or Akshar) of the season to the gods and goddesses. This uncooked rice is used in auspicious occasions such as weddings and is known as Akshata, the finest offering one can make. Then they offer payasam with milk and white rice to Goddess Annapurna.

A World of Wheat

Raghu exclaimed, 'What a nice story, Ajji! We all eat rice, but I had never heard the story of how it came to be on earth.'

Anoushka replied, 'I don't like rice at all, but I love rotis. When we were living in Delhi, our school's canteen would have different types of rotis on offer. How did wheat come to earth, Ajji?'

Ajji looked at the children, but her mind wandered elsewhere.

'Ajji is a treasure trove of stories. I am sure she knows this story too,' said Ajja, his face crinkling into a slight smile.

'Yes, of course I know. Kamlu Ajji knows the same one too. Kamlu, why don't you tell them this story?'

'Maybe I will share it tomorrow, you must all be tired now,' said Kamlu Ajji.

'No, Kamlu Ajji, we are never too tired to hear stories. Please tell us,' insisted Meenu.

And so, Kamlu Ajji began her story.

Arun was a young, brave and courageous lad. He loved adventures, so he decided to set out from his village. He took his bow and arrows and began walking aimlessly—he wanted to explore the world.

After trekking for a few hundred kilometres, he came across a beautiful lake with a bridge. As he got closer, he saw a huge serpent occupying the entire length of the bridge. He had two choices: he could either turn back or cross the bridge regardless of the serpent. If he chose the latter, he would have to step on the serpent carefully until he reached the other end.

Since Arun didn't want to go back, he began walking on the serpent's body. After he took a few strides, he heard a voice say, 'Hello, hello, stop right there!'

Arun turned around and to his astonishment, he saw that the serpent had vanished and in its place stood an old man. A little afraid, he asked the old man, 'Are you calling out to me?'

'Yes.'

'Where is the serpent? It was here a moment ago,' asked Arun.

'I am the serpent. In fact, I am the king of serpents and have a fantastic palace below this lake,' said the old man.

'Then why were you sleeping here?'

'To see if I could solve a problem. You see, there is a cruel and powerful eagle who lives on the other side of the mountain. Every day, she comes and eats

one of my subjects. Besides my subjects, I have many children, grandchildren and great-grandchildren too, and no matter how much I try, I have not been able to defeat the eagle. So, I wanted to test and find someone who is bold and courageous, and will agree to help us. That is why I changed my size and laid down on the bridge. Everybody who came here chose to turn back, except you. You have passed my test. Will you try and help us?'

Hearing the sincerity in the old man's voice, Arun knew instantly that he was telling the truth. The desire to help save a kingdom and to fight a nasty eagle was too strong for Arun to refuse. He nodded.

The old man smiled, relieved to have found a ray of hope. 'We have some time before the eagle comes again tomorrow. Would you like to visit my palace?' he asked.

Arun agreed and they both jumped into the water.

Arun thought that he would hit bottom soon, but he didn't. The two men passed through a tunnel and entered a beautiful, impressive city with plenty of plants, fruits and flowers. Many serpents walked around in the form of humans, but there was a stillness in the water. Despite the obvious prosperity, no one seemed happy.

The serpent king guided Arun to his palace. Soon, there was a huge feast laid out in his honour. There was more food than he had ever seen before! After a hearty meal, the king introduced him to his clan.

The king thought, *Poor Arun, this might be his last meal.*

The next morning, the serpent king and Arun came back to the surface of the lake.

It wasn't long before Arun heard a terrifying screech. An enormous and scary eagle was heading towards them, intent on breaking through the water and finding its next victim from the city that lay underneath.

Arun took out his bow and got ready to shoot at the eagle. He only had three arrows in his quiver.

He shot the first arrow—it touched the left wing of the eagle, broke and fell down. The eagle continued flying without missing a beat. The serpent king grew concerned. *Perhaps this boy will not be able to slay the eagle either*, he thought.

He let loose the second arrow—it touched the right wing of the eagle, broke and fell down. The eagle continued to fly steadily towards them. The serpent king grew more and more concerned.

There was only one arrow left now, and the eagle was going to reach them soon.

Arun looked down at the lake and saw the eagle's reflection in the water. There was a wound on the eagle's neck. Arun took aim, said a prayer and launched an arrow directly at the eagle's wound. The arrow hit its mark, and the eagle collapsed into the water and drowned.

The cruel eagle had finally been slain.

The serpent king was ecstatic. He embraced Arun, 'My child, thank you for your kindness and bravery. I can never repay your favour, nor will my kingdom or my subjects ever forget you.'

The city and all the serpent folk celebrated the victory with gusto. The king took Arun on a personal tour of the kingdom. Arun noticed that in every home, people were cooking something he had never seen before — it was cream and beige in colour.

The serpents requested him to stay in the city for some time, but Arun wanted to go and explore more of the world. At the farewell lunch on the final day of his stay, Arun noticed that the same thing he had seen being cooked earlier was being served in different varieties.

'What is this?' he asked.

'This is wheat, it originates from grass. We only eat the grain we obtain from it during festivals or on special occasions like today. We are honouring you by serving wheat,' explained the king.

The queen joined in and said, 'We make a variety of dishes using wheat, it is a vital food and easy to eat and digest. It also gives us lots of energy.'

Arun tried it and enjoyed it more than anything else that had been served.

When he was about to leave, the queen came and presented him with bags of gold nuggets, diamonds, rubies and emeralds. The king said, 'This is our gift to you.'

However, Arun politely refused the gift. He said, 'I don't need these expensive stones or metals. If you really want to give me something, please give me a handful of wheat seeds that I can plant and help my fellow men enjoy it too!'

The king and queen exchanged looks, they had never shared this with any human before. The serpent king said, 'Gratitude is the highest representation of civilization. We will share some wheat seeds with you and teach you how to grow it. Let your world also enjoy this. Whenever you eat wheat, remember that we shared our secret with you and that you helped us through a tough time.'

The king handed over a bag of wheat seeds and soon, Arun left the serpent kingdom and returned to land, bringing the secret of wheat along with him.

The Magic Beans/Jaggu
and the Beanstalk

The next morning, Ajji called the children and said, 'The lockdown has begun. We should obey the prime minister and do what our country needs. Each of you must wash your hands multiple times a day and avoid touching your face, mouth and nose with your hands. If you feel unwell, tell me immediately.'

'No helpers will come to work in our house from today,' added Ajja. 'That means we have to help Ajji.'

'Yes,' said Ajji. 'Now, I will rely on you to help around the house, and chores will be assigned to everyone. Kamlu will look after the kitchen and I will monitor the running of the household.'

The children nodded, slightly anxious but unable to fully comprehend the seriousness of the lockdown.

Ajji gave clear instructions: 'Raghu, you will help Ajja clean and vacuum the house. Krishna will help with the dishwashing. Anoushka and Aditi will help me with the laundry. Meenu, you will assist Kamlu Ajji in the kitchen and gather and wash vegetables too.'

'You never know, kids. You might find it fun to work together!' said Ajja, trying to lighten the mood as he saw their worried faces.

The children nodded and split up to take care of their chores.

Meenu went with Kamlu Ajji to gather vegetables from the garden. She was very happy to see tomatoes, pumpkins, greens and different types of gourds. But there were no cabbages, cauliflowers or potatoes.

'Look at the beans!' exclaimed Kamlu Ajji. 'They are fresh. Go ahead, Meenu, pick them from the bush. It is very easy. Today, we will eat tomato rice and roti with a sabzi made of beans.'

Meenu started gathering the beans and soon, her basket was full. They came home and Meenu began washing the beans in the kitchen sink.

Everyone was busy working in the house—cleaning, cooking, washing dishes or doing laundry.

Once the chores were done, the children gathered to play and saw that Ajji was in an animated discussion with Ajja for a long time. After some time, she announced, 'Kids, it is important to help others at this time. Ajja and I are thinking of making dry ration kits, so that we can give them to people who can't afford it but will need it during the lockdown period. Each kit will contain rations for twenty-one days. Rehmat Chacha will come home in his jeep to pick up the kits, but we can't let him inside because we must practise social distancing. We will keep the kits by the gate and he will pick them up.'

'This activity will add more work for us,' said Ajja. 'But we have a solution. Vishnu Kaka is out of station and his trusted helper Damu is alone in the house next door. I spoke to them both. Damu will come in the mornings, help us with packing and household chores and go back in the evenings to Kaka's house to sleep. He will not go anywhere else. Since Damu is alone, he quite liked the idea of being with us.'

Ajji smiled at Ajja and said, 'Come, let's eat lunch and start packing!'

After lunch, Raghu said, 'I want to sit down and relax for a few minutes. Why don't we all take a break? You can tell us a story, Ajji!'

'The story can wait, Raghu, but hunger cannot. Come, let's sit and pack. Will you help me?' asked Ajji.

'We will all help, Ajji,' clamoured the children.

My Ajji is very nice and kind. I like it that helping others is more important to her than other things, thought Krishna, feeling proud of her grandmother.

Just then, Damu entered the house. He greeted the children quickly and helped Ajji bring out huge bags of rice, dal, oil bottles, salt and sugar along with packets of masalas from the storeroom. Ajji had got these from the market two days ago. Each child grabbed a bag to work with and started putting the ingredients into smaller one-kilo bags.

Ajja or Ajji carried a medium-sized cardboard box to the children, and they each added one small bag of their ingredient to it. Once all the items were in the box, Damu packed it and kept it next to the main gate. The children really enjoyed making the small packets and didn't think of it as work at all. Time passed quickly and soon it was early evening. Ajja counted the boxes and announced, 'We have made two hundred boxes!'

Soon, Rehmat Chacha also came and quickly loaded the boxes in his jeep and took them away to be distributed. The children were excited and felt happy about lending a hand. 'Give us more! We want to do more!' said Krishna.

'Yes, yes, we do,' said Meenu.

'I want to call and tell my mother how much I have helped!' screamed Anoushka.

'We have done a lot of work for the day. I have ordered more rations, which will be here by tomorrow, so let's stop for now and continue tomorrow,' replied Ajja.

After they had cleaned up, the children gathered around Ajji as she was washing her hands, 'Tell us a story now!'

'Maybe I will tell you after dinner,' said Ajji.

'I am still full from lunch,' said Raghu.

Anoushka said, 'Me too! The beans sabzi was excellent. I ate three bowls.'

'It was so easy to pluck them from the bush too!' said Meenu. 'Perhaps we can pluck more tomorrow. But if Kamlu Ajji tells me to get coconuts, I can't get those by myself, they are too high.'

'Why are coconuts found at the top of a tree, while beans grow in shrubs?' wondered Raghu.

'There is a reason for that,' said Ajji, wiping her hands.

'What reason?' asked Raghu.

'It all began with a beanstalk,' said Ajji, as she sat down and began her story.

Anita and Jaggu lived on a farm. Anita worked hard, but her husband was very lazy. She would tell her husband every day, 'If you help me, we can do a lot together. I can't do everything by myself. We are poor farmers. Please lend a hand so that we can lead a better life.'

Jaggu, however, wouldn't listen. Poor Anita did whatever she could. She worked hard to grow vegetables and sold them at the market. The money was just enough to make ends meet and somehow, Anita managed to take care of the house and their basic needs.

One day, while returning from the market, there was loud thunder and a heavy downpour. Anita was passing by a small house and decided to ask for shelter there. She saw an old man cooking, he invited her to sit down in the veranda and wait for the rain to stop. When the rain showed no signs of stopping, the man said, 'Please come inside, young lady. Have a meal before you go.'

Anita was thankful for his kindness and gave him the leftover vegetables she was carrying back home. The rain refused to subside. While speaking to each other, Anita told the man about the farm and her problems. She didn't have anyone with whom she could share her deepest thoughts and problems, and she felt comfortable in the company of this sweet and gentle old man.

He smiled and listened to her carefully.

After another hour, the rain stopped. Before she left, the old man gave her one seed of a bean. He said, 'Anita, this is an unusual seed. Grow this and you will get a delicious vegetable. You can sell it in the market. This will fetch you more money since it will be a new kind of vegetable.'

Anita thanked the old man, took the seed and went home.

The next day, she planted the seed. Within a month, the seed grew into a creeper. Green beans began sprouting around it and shot upwards, but only till Anita's hands could reach when she stood on tiptoe. The creeper, however, kept going up and up—so high that Anita couldn't see where it ended.

Since the vegetable was new and delicious, people bought her produce very quickly and she was able to sell all of it. Anita was happy with her earnings and was grateful for the good food and the repairs she could now do around the house.

Now, lazy Jaggu became very curious about these new beans. He started getting up early, not to help his wife but to see and monitor the beanstalk. 'How tall do you think the stalk is?' he asked.

'I don't know and I am not interested. I get enough beans to sell at the market,' she replied.

Jaggu, however, kept pestering her. 'Ask that old man to give you some more seeds,' he suggested. 'There are no seeds in these beans. But if the old man gives you some, we can plant many more and get rich.'

'No, I am content with what we have now. Don't be greedy, Jaggu. We have enough.'

Jaggu gave up on her and went in search of the old man. The day that Anita had brought the seed

31

home, she had told him about the house where she had met him. Soon enough, Jaggu found the house. But to his dismay, there was nobody inside.

Perhaps I should climb the beanstalk instead and see how far up it goes, he thought. *But I can't do it when Anita is at home. She will surely try to stop me.*

So, he returned home and waited for Anita to leave the house. After a few days, Anita went to the market to sell the beans. The moment she left, Jaggu began climbing the beanstalk.

After what seemed like hours, he reached the top and followed a trail to a house in the clouds.

The door was closed.

He knocked. *Knock-knock-knock.*

A man's voice asked, 'Who is it? Why have you come here?'

'Sir, I am Anita's husband, Jaggu.'

'What do you want?'

Jaggu hesitated. *Why should I ask for more beans?* he thought. *More beans means I'll have to work hard and only then will I get the money. I'd rather ask for money straight away.*

So he said, 'Money. I want money.'

'Sure,' said the voice. 'Now go away.'

Jaggu went back to the beanstalk and climbed down all the way to the bottom. When he entered his house, he saw a box overflowing with money. Suddenly, he felt disappointed. 'I should have asked for gold nuggets instead of money,' he thought. 'It would have been worth much more.'

Anita came back home, but he didn't tell her what had happened that day. Instead, he managed to get by with the money for a few days and waited for her to go to the market again so that he could climb up the beanstalk and ask for gold nuggets this time.

But soon, he changed his mind. *What is the use of nuggets?* he thought to himself. *Those are not important either. I must become the richest man in the village. That is the best way to trick the man who lives up there.*

The next time Anita went to the market, Jaggu climbed the beanstalk again. He reached the top and followed the trail to the house in the clouds.

The door was closed.

He knocked. *Knock-knock-knock.*

A man's voice asked, 'Who is it? Why have you come here?'

'Sir, I am Anita's husband, Jaggu.'

'What do you want?'

'I want to be the richest person in the village.'

'Sure,' said the voice. 'Now go away, and don't come here again.'

33

Jaggu climbed down, feeling happy and carefree. He knew he was going to be the richest person in the village, and he was.

This time, he told Anita what had happened when she came back home. Anita wasn't pleased.

'I don't want to participate or use the money that you have received in this way. Do what you want, but leave me out of it,' she replied.

Jaggu was least bothered. He began wondering what he should do now that he was rich. He began inviting other rich people of the village to his house for meals.

Anita refused to join in and continued her work quietly.

One day, Jaggu hosted a big dinner for all his new friends in his new palatial house. However, they declined because they had another invitation for the same day. All of them said, 'The king is coming to the village. So we must accept his dinner invitation first.'

That means that the king is more powerful than the rich! he thought. *Perhaps I should go back and ask that man on top of the beanstalk to make me powerful.*

The next time Anita went out, Jaggu climbed the beanstalk again. He reached the top and followed the trail to the house in the clouds.

The door was closed.

He knocked. *Knock-knock-knock.*

A man's voice asked, 'Who is it? Why have you come here?'

'Sir, I am Anita's husband, Jaggu.'

'What do you want?'

'I want to become the most powerful king in the land.'

'Sure,' said the voice. 'Now go away, and don't come here again.'

Jaggu's wish was granted once again, and he became the most powerful king in the land. Anita, however, refused to become queen and stayed back in her house. She continued growing and selling the beans.

One day, Jaggu asked her, 'We have so much money that seven generations can live and thrive on it. Why do you still work so hard?'

Anita knew that her husband's greedy and lazy nature would make him pay a heavy price one day. Out loud, she said, 'Your status has been earned through magic while mine has been through hard work. Mine will remain with me forever.'

Jaggu shook his head, unable to comprehend the truth in his wife's words.

One day, Jaggu went to meet the emperor of the land. The minister said, 'Please wait, he can't meet you now.'

'Why? What is he doing?' demanded Jaggu.

'He is praying and performing a puja.'

'Does he do this every day?' asked Jaggu.

'Yes, sir, every morning. God is the most powerful of all and everyone must bow down to his divine presence,' said the minister.

Even the emperor must bow down to God. So why don't I become God? he thought.

So the next time Anita went out, Jaggu went back to his old house and climbed the beanstalk again. He reached the top and followed the trail to the house in the clouds.

The door was closed.

He knocked. *Knock-knock-knock*.

A man's voice asked, 'Who is it? Why have you come here?'

'Sir, I am Anita's husband, Jaggu.'

'What do you want?' asked the voice, sounding angry.

'I promise I won't come again if you make me God. I want to become God. Please,' pleaded Jaggu.

The voice laughed heartily.

'Ha ha ha! God is everywhere in the universe. He is kind and compassionate, and an individual can attain godliness only by doing great work. You are a greedy and lazy fellow and I have had it with your wishes! You deserve nothing!'

Jaggu felt an invisible kick to his rear end and he fell down from the clouds. He landed in the front yard of his small house. There were bruises everywhere on his body. The beanstalk disappeared and only the shrub remained with the beans that Anita had grown. Disappointed and hurt, Jaggu went inside his tiny house.

When Anita came home, she was shocked to see her wounded husband and a small shrub in the front yard. The beanstalk had vanished too! She realized what had happened. Worried that she would run out of beans, she went to the shrub and plucked a bean. To her surprise, this time, the beans had seeds.

'What happened?' she demanded.

Jaggu told her the entire story.

'You deserve this,' remarked Anita. 'When you don't work hard for your living, you don't value what you receive. You have forgotten that we are farmers. Our duty is to farm and enjoy our produce. God has taught you a good lesson. Now, forget the past and

Sudha Murty

come with me. I will tend to your bruises. Despite everything, God is kind. He has given us seeds so we can replicate them and continue to earn enough money.'

Anita opened her box of savings. She said, 'This is all that I could save. Let us use this money to work hard and plant more bean shrubs. It is God's gift to us and as long as we take care of it and use it wisely, we will have enough.'

Thus, Jaggu mended his ways and together, the couple grew a lot of beans and led a healthy and content life.

Even today, beans grow in shrubs and not in beanstalks that reach the sky.

'Wow, is that really why beans grow in shrubs, Ajji?' asked Anoushka, wide-eyed.

'Nobody knows for sure, but I always believed this story to be true,' said Ajji.

'Beans are my new favourite vegetable,' announced Meenu.

Ajji gave her an affectionate look and smiled.

The Goddess of Luck

A few days later, Rehmat Chacha called up Ajja and said, 'Thank you for the food kits. It is all being distributed today and will help a lot of people. I have also received several requests for masks from many people. Will you be able to help with that too? If you can, please let me know. We can pick them up and distribute them in the slums.'

'I will check and call you back, Rehmat,' assured Ajja as he kept the phone down. He turned to Ajji, 'What do you think? Do we have the material to make masks?'

'Of course. I know how to make them, but I need cloth of a comfortable and breathable material,' said Ajji. Suddenly, she recalled, 'I bought a lot of dhotis a few weeks ago to distribute to people during the cart festival. That material is comfortable and easy to wash. I can use that to make masks. We can start doing that today. If they want more, tell Rehmat to bring some more material and keep it outside the house. We'll leave it in the garden for twenty-four hours. Then I will pick it up and use that as well.'

Kamlu Ajji joined her. Her work had been eased because Damu was helping her with the household chores, even though she was still the main cook. The children were helping, but they still needed a lot of monitoring, which was not always possible. Damu's presence was of great help to both the Ajjis.

Kamlu Ajji said, 'Come, let's work on it together after lunch. I will cut the material and you can stitch. This way, it will be faster.'

'That's a wonderful idea,' said Ajji.

All the children gathered around the sewing machine after lunch, but nobody wanted to ask Ajji to tell a story. Ajja called out from the room next door, 'Ajji cannot tell a story today because she has to focus on the stitching. So does Kamlu Ajji. So I will tell you a story.'

The children ran to their grandfather's room, all excited. It was an old room, like him. It had tall ceilings and an ancient fan. Ajja sat on a cosy chair.

'You? You can tell us a story?' asked Raghu, slightly astonished. Ajja had never told them a story before.

'Yes, of course I can, Raghu. After all, I am married to Ajji, am I not? Come, sit!' winked Ajja.

The room was nice and comfortable and the children sat around him in anticipation.

Ajja began, 'I am only telling you this story so you realize how important it is to lend a hand. When we help others, things happen the way they should— almost as if someone is helping you too!'

'What does that mean, Ajja?' asked Meenu.

Ajja smiled.

Mahesh and his wife lived in a village with their two daughters. Though both husband and wife worked hard, they barely managed to make ends meet. Mahesh was always worried about money for his daughters' education and their future. He attempted many things to make money, but failed time and again. He thought that luck was not on his side.

One day, Mahesh had a dream. A man came to him and said, 'Mahesh, pray to the goddess of luck,

Adrushtalakshmi. If you pray to her, she will remove all obstacles in your way and help you prosper.'

'Where do I find her?' asked Mahesh.

'You must go deep into the forest, climb a big mountain you'll find there and meditate. She will come and help you.'

When he woke up the next morning, Mahesh told his wife about the dream and she encouraged him to follow the instructions. The same day, Mahesh set out for the forest.

On his journey, he saw two horses, they were hungry and upset.

Mahesh sat under a tree nearby and ate his lunch. He shared whatever he had with the horses. They asked, 'O young man, where are you going?'

'I am in search of the goddess of luck. I have been unlucky in many adventures and would like the boon of luck from her,' replied Mahesh.

'Will you ask her something for us? We have been here for several years. It is hard to find food and we are tired. Wherever we go, we encounter wild animals and there is barely any grass around. If you meet the goddess, ask her where we can get good grassland so that we can move there. That is all we want.'

Mahesh nodded, saddened by the plight of the horses.

He walked for a long time until he ran into an almost-dead mango tree. Mahesh sat under it and later, slept in its shade for some time. When he was about to resume his journey, the mango tree asked, 'O young man, where are you going?'

Mahesh explained his mission.

'Will you ask the goddess a favour on my behalf? All my siblings are healthy and give juicy fruits. Humans, animals and birds really enjoy their fruits. I was born with them, but as you can see, I am half-dead and half alive. I have no flowers and no fruits to give, no matter how much I try. I feel that my life has no purpose. Can anything be done for me?'

Mahesh promised to ask the goddess and moved on.

Then he came across the mountain that the man in his dream had mentioned. He climbed and climbed until he reached a pond. Many birds were crying around a dry lake. They asked him, 'O young man, where are you going?'

Mahesh explained his mission.

The birds said, 'We always get rain most of the year, and we can all drink water from the lake. But look at it now! It dries up every summer. Somehow, we can manage to get food, but water is very hard to get.

43

Sudha Murty

Will you ask the goddess if there is any way to get water throughout the year?'

Mahesh promised and continued his journey. At last, he reached the top of the mountain. There, he began to pray sincerely.

After a long time, the goddess of luck appeared. She said, 'Mahesh, I am happy with your devotion. You have come all the way through the forest and climbed a difficult mountain. I can bless you with three boons. Please ask.'

Suddenly, Mahesh thought of the horses with no grass to eat. He remembered the mango tree and the suffering of the birds. He said, 'Mother, on this journey to find you, I have come across beings in three difficult situations. Please tell me how to solve their problems.'

She smiled and said, 'I know.' She continued, 'Their problems are simple to solve. In the area where the horses reside, there is a stone under a tree. The stone can only be removed by a person who is pure of heart and who thinks of everyone's happiness. If such a person removes the stone, the area will be filled with grass that will last the horses a lifetime!'

Mahesh looked at her with love and admiration, wondering how she knew the details of his journey.

'Below the mango tree,' she said, 'there is a box. Remove it and the tree will bear more fruits and flowers than any other tree around it. There is another box near the side of the lake where the birds reside. Dig the box out and the water will remain in the lake throughout the year.'

'Remember, Mahesh, carry the boxes back to your home and open them in the company of your wife.'

Mahesh was happy to hear the solutions. He thanked the goddess and started on his return journey.

First, he reached the lake. There, he removed the box easily and instantly, and water began flowing into the lake. The birds cheered and thanked him. Mahesh quickly went on his way.

Next, Mahesh went to the mango tree and removed a big box from the ground. The mango tree thanked him and Mahesh continued on his journey back home.

Finally, he met the horses and noticed a big stone under one of the trees nearby. He wondered, *Where will I find a virtuous person to remove this big stone? There is nobody here but me. Let me try.*

To his surprise, he was able to remove the stone with ease and just as suddenly, he saw the grass begin to sprout. He had never thought of himself as pure of heart, but the goddess of luck knew that he hadn't asked anything for himself, but for others. Then who could be more virtuous than him?

At last, Mahesh reached home and narrated the events of his journey to his wife.

'What's in these boxes?' she asked, puzzled.

'I didn't open them, dear. The goddess wanted us to open them together,' he said.

When they opened the boxes, they found gold in one box and diamonds in the other. Mahesh cried out with happiness and knew that he would be able to take better care of his daughters and give them an excellent education.

That is how the goddess of luck always knows how to choose a good person.

A Sibling Story

Whenever Ajja put the television on, there were more updates about Covid-19 cases and the lockdown statuses in different states. Things were looking bleaker than before as cases were on the rise.

One morning, Ajja woke up with a pain in one of his legs. Usually, he massaged some oil on his leg by himself. It always helped him feel better. But today, Kamlu Ajji insisted on bringing the oil in a bowl.

'Put your legs on my lap,' she ordered him.

Ajja obediently did as told.

Kamlu Ajji began massaging the leg that was hurting. Her face softened. 'Do you remember how I used to massage you when you had back pain during your younger days?'

Ajja nodded. He looked like a small child with his legs sprawled over his sister's lap. The children found it amusing. 'Ajja, you are old, but you look like you are one of us,' giggled Meenu and made fun of him.

'A brother and sister's relationship is a very sweet one and celebrated all over India,' said Ajji, coming to Ajja's rescue.

'Yes,' added Ajja. 'Every year, Kamlu and I exchange gifts on a certain festival. Do you know which festival I am talking about?'

'Are you talking about Raksha Bandhan?' asked Raghu. 'It is such a big festival and Meenu always takes a big gift from me and gives me a small rakhi.'

Ajja smiled. 'It is not about a big gift or the small delicate thread of rakhi. The thread is meant to reassure your sister that you will always be with her when she is facing difficult times. Even history recognizes

the significance of this festival. It is believed that Rani Karnavati sent a rakhi to the Mughal emperor Humayun when enemies were trying to attack, and Humayun rushed in to protect her. But I am not talking about the thread of rakhi here.'

'Then what festival are you referring to?' asked Anoushka.

'Naga Panchami,' said Ajja. His eyes twinkled and he turned to Ajji. 'Come on, tell the children the story behind why we celebrate Naga Panchami in the south and Bhaubeej in Maharashtra.'

Ajji smiled and began narrating the story.

One day, the king of Avanti was travelling on horseback and decided to take a break after hours of riding.

He sat on a big stone that lay on the side of the road and took out his bottle of water to drink. Suddenly, his eyes fell on a stone under his feet—it was in the shape of a snake and was red in colour. It fascinated him because he had never seen anything like it. *This looks precious and unique*, he thought.

He picked it up and brought it back to the palace. Once he was home, he gave it to his wife and told her to keep it safe.

The next day, he told the queen to open the box that held the stone. To their surprise, a handsome prince with a beautiful turban came out of the box. There was a big red jewel on top of his turban.

The queen, shocked and bewildered, asked, 'Who are you? Why are you here?'

The prince smiled. 'Do not ask me questions, Your Highness. Tell me what you want done, and I will make sure it happens.

The king hesitated. However, the queen did not. She said, 'There is a wretched asura that lives near a mountain in our kingdom. He is the cause of a lot of trouble to our subjects and though we have tried, it seems to be impossible to kill him. Prince, if you can help with this, I will be grateful.'

'Give me a horse and a sword,' said the prince. 'That is more than enough. I can manage the rest.'

The king agreed but also insisted on sending a few soldiers with him.

When the group reached the bottom of the mountain, the asura appeared, ready to fight. The prince

fought him alone and within a few minutes, he managed to slay the terrible asura.

Within hours, the prince and the troupe were back in the king's palace.

The prince was humble about his victory, but the soldiers accompanying him described the sequence of events and his extraordinary valour.

A month passed and soon the soldiers from a neighbouring land invaded the kingdom. The prince said to the king, 'Don't worry, sire. I will take care of this problem.'

Alone, he fought them all and defeated the enemy.

With that, the news about the brave prince spread to different lands and nobody dared to invade the kingdom again.

In the meantime, the king had a beautiful daughter who had fallen in love with the prince. She shared her desire to marry him, but the king refused. He said, 'No, my child. The prince is handsome and a great warrior, but we know very little about him. How can I give my daughter to an unknown prince?'

The princess insisted, 'But, Father, I refuse to marry anyone else.'

Time passed and the king realized that his daughter would not change her mind. He gave up and arranged for the wedding of the couple with the prince's consent.

One day, there was a festival in the kingdom. All the brides wore their best clothing and the finest jewellery and gathered in the palace. A bride said, 'My mother-in-law has sent me this sari!' Another one said, 'I got this bangle from my husband's sister!'

Suddenly, the princess felt sad. Everything she had or was wearing was given by her father or mother—she hadn't received a gift from her husband or his parents. She felt so insecure at this sudden discovery that she became disheartened and sad. That night, she asked her husband, 'Tell me more about yourself. Where are your parents? Do you have any siblings? I would love to meet them. I want to show everyone that you have a family that cares about us!'

The prince smiled and said, 'Don't ask me these questions. Leave things as they are.'

But she didn't. The princess hounded him day and night.

One day, the couple went for a picnic near the river. The princess went into the water and all of a sudden, was in a terrible mood. She turned to the prince with a determined look in her eyes and threatened, 'Tell me who your parents are. Otherwise, I will drown myself.'

The prince, tired of her questioning, said, 'You don't need to die and I cannot answer your questions.'

He jumped into the water and drowned himself. The turban along with the red jewel disappeared somewhere under the water.

The princess was shocked! She burst out crying. He had never told her who he was and her stubbornness had gotten in her own way. She felt stupid at her silly actions that had caused her to lose her husband. For the next few months, she neither ate nor slept properly.

A friend who lived near the same river came to visit her one day and said, 'Princess, I had a very interesting experience yesterday. I still don't know for certain whether it was a dream or it was me being half asleep as I rested in my garden at home. It was quite warm outside in the evening when I saw a snake coming out of the river. It drew a big circle on the ground and transformed into a man. Many other snakes followed suit and took the form of humans. Then, some of them laid a carpet on the floor and finally, a king and a prince arrived with their entourage. The prince had a red stone on his majestic turban, but he looked very pale. I couldn't see clearly, but he reminded me of your husband.

'The men and women began talking to each other. One of the women said, "The prince had to stay on earth for some time as punishment because he lost his stone, but since he has returned from land, he is unhappy. In fact, he is downright miserable. Even his beloved sister Maya hasn't been able to cheer him up!"

"'Why doesn't he go back there?" someone else suggested.

"'He can't go on his own. Someone has to pull him out from the circle."

'The discussion died down. They all danced and partied for some time, and then they changed back into snakes and returned to the river.'

The dream made the princess realize that her husband was the prince of serpents who lived underwater. She decided to go with her friend to the same location the next day.

Once the princess had reached that spot, she hid behind a bush and waited to see if the snakes would appear again.

Soon enough, the snakes appeared with their king and prince, turned into men and women and the party began in a marked circle. The prince, her husband, stood all alone in one corner. He was near her. The princess saw her chance and pulled him out of the circle with a sudden jerk of her hand.

The music stopped. The merry dance stopped. Everyone stared at her. The prince smiled at her with love.

The princess bowed low to the king of the serpents, 'Sire, please excuse me. I love my husband, and I know that it was wrong on my part to insist on learning about his background. He was unable to tell me the truth, but I know everything now. My husband loves me a lot and that is why he has been dejected since his return. Please, I urge you, allow us to live happily and in peace. As a mark of respect and love for your gesture, we will celebrate a festival in your honour for two days and feed you and your subjects milk. We will call you Naga Devata, and you will be equal to the status of a god.'

'No!' cried Maya. 'You can't take my brother to the land of humans.'

'But he can always come to visit you!' said the princess.

The prince shook his head.

'No, it is not allowed,' said Maya. 'If he goes back, he will lose the citizenship of our kingdom. My brother and I are very close, and we are always there for each other. I cannot let him go to your land forever!'

The king, however, smiled and with a wave of his hand, he silenced Maya.

He said to the princess, 'My dear girl, I appreciate your courage and your true love for the prince. Had you failed in your attempt to get your husband back, you would have had a difficult life ahead. As an exception, I will allow my son to be the subject of both kingdoms, as long as he continues to serve wherever he is. He can visit us whenever he needs us. You have one husband, but I have many children. I will manage to run the kingdom. May God bless you!'

The princess thanked the king profusely and turned to Maya, 'You can come and visit your brother whenever you want. It will be wonderful to have you with us.'

'I have much work to do here, but I will come and see my brother for two days every year,' said Maya, smiling at her.

Thus, the prince went back to land and stayed with the princess. Together, they led a long and a happy life.

From that day, two days a year in the rainy season are dedicated to the worship of snakes. This festival is known as Naga Panchami, and it is a custom for sisters to visit their brothers' homes during this time.

A Handful of Grains

The children were now getting used to a new life. They were learning to tackle the challenges life posed and were helping each other as the days progressed.

The next morning, Anoushka's chores included bringing flowers from the garden for Ajji. When she went to the garden, she saw a beautiful rose. Then her eyes fell on a jasmine flower, and then *champaka* flowers growing on a tree! She thought of climbing the tree but a few seconds later, she saw *bakula* flowers on the ground and gave up! She got confused about which flowers to pick and sat on the ground, staring at the beautiful choices of flowers around her.

Twenty minutes later, Ajji walked into the garden looking for her. 'Did you finish gathering the flowers?' she asked.

'I wanted to, but . . .'

'What happened?'

'My hand started to hurt . . .' Anoushka tried to make an excuse. 'No, I meant my leg started to hurt!'

'Really?' grimaced Ajji, knowing full well that Anoushka was not suffering any pain at all. 'Should I tell Kamlu Ajji to massage your leg?'

'No, no,' replied Anoushka quickly.

'You don't pick flowers with your leg. I know you are making excuses. Come now, you aren't Champa.'

'Who is Champa?' asked Anoushka.

'I'll tell you all a quick story, but then you must gather the flowers, Anoushka. After that, I must go finish some other work,' said Ajji.

Anoushka nodded her head vigorously and called out to all the other children. She yelled, 'Come, come. Ajji is telling us a story. You can help me gather the flowers while she is talking.'

Champa was a little girl who lived in a village with her parents. She would spend most of her time playing with a little mouse called Mini. Her mother would often get upset at this. She would scold her, 'Why are you wasting your time with a little mouse? After all, it is a small animal that is of no use.'

Champa, however, would never listen. One day, while playing with Mini, her mother called out to her and said, 'Champa, it is almost time for lunch. Bring me some dry wood from the backyard. I can only cook after you bring me the wood.'

Champa was hungry, so she immediately went to the backyard to fetch some wood. But alas! The wood there was half wet. There was no dry wood at all!

'Why is the wood wet even in this scorching summer?' Champa wondered aloud.

To her surprise, a log of wood spoke to her, 'Oh Champa, I would have dried and been of some use to your family, but look at the grass around me! It hasn't been cut or cleared in ages. That is why there's always shade here and the sun's rays don't reach me at all!'

Champa was surprised at the log's words and she glanced down at the grass surrounding the wood. It was true!

The moment she looked at the grass, the grass spoke, 'Oh! What can I do? I don't get the sun's rays either, and that is why I am wet.'

Champa looked up at the sky. The sun was not shining brightly, and said, 'I wish I could send enough heat to reach the grass. But the clouds are blocking my rays.'

Champa now understood what was going on. She looked at the cloud. 'I wish I could move ahead and allow the sun's rays through,' said the clouds. 'But the wind blows me this way.'

She looked at the wind, who said, 'I am sorry, but I'm helpless. Your king has built such a big palace that it has forced me to change my direction. Moreover, he has blocked the door right at the top of the palace. If he opens the door, I can pass.'

In the far distance, Champa saw the king standing on a balcony in the palace. She could see the shadow of a door at the top. She looked at the king, who said, 'I wish I could open that door, but the queen hasn't given me permission to do so.'

Champa looked at the queen. She was sitting near the door with a parrot nearby. The queen said, 'That is my special room and I don't have time to open the door because I am busy listening to the stories of this parrot, who has come from a distant land.'

Champa looked at the parrot—the bird was so different and beautiful. Usually, parrots are green with red beaks. This parrot, however, was multicoloured. For a few seconds, she forgot herself and stared at the parrot. The parrot said, 'I live in a land far, far away on a green tree that has plenty of flowers and fruits through the year. One branch of the tree is bent very close to the water in a lake. The lord of the lake scares me. He keeps threatening to drown the branch. So, I flew away in search of a home, and came here. I know countless stories and I have seen beautiful things. So I stay, tell stories and describe those things to the queen. Still, home is home and I miss it.'

Champa thought of the land far, far away and the lake that the parrot had mentioned. Suddenly, the lake and its lord appeared in her vision. The lord said, 'I am always in danger from an elephant who threatens to drink all my water and turn me dry every time he is upset. So I get frustrated and I am mean to the little bird that sits near me on the branch of the tree.'

Champa's thoughts turned to the elephant. He appeared in her mind, worried. He said, 'I am a gentle vegetarian and I like to keep to myself most of the time. I like to spend time with my family and I don't have any enemies. Though I have might, I don't use it unless it is required. Unfortunately, there is a serpent that wants to bite me. He sits on my tail sometimes and I can't get him off me no matter what I do. He hisses and intimidates me so much. I am not upset with the lake, but on some days, I just want to go into the lake and drown myself in its waters. I want to drink all the water and spray it on my whole body in the hope that the serpent will wash away. In my heart, I love the lake. It gives me cool water, especially during the summer. But I don't know how else to try and get rid of the serpent.'

Champa was surprised. Even the mighty elephant was scared of a serpent. The serpent then appeared in her thoughts and started to shed tears. He said, 'I don't want to harm anyone. I enjoy living far from civilization, but people want to kill me the moment they see me. Besides, I am a non-poisonous snake, but my size is huge. There is a mouse in a potter's shop nearby and I would love to eat it and satiate my hunger, but she disappears so quickly. She is the only mouse I have seen in this area. I can eat other things, but eating a mouse is a feast. Every time I try to find her, the potter comes with a stick and tries to slaughter me. That's when I get scared and find refuge on the elephant's tail. A potter is no match to an elephant's strength.'

Champa then thought of the potter. He was speaking to his wife, 'The serpent has ruined all the work that I did this month. Just the other day, I found him hiding under the pots. I tried to shoo him away, but he upset my pots and broke most of them. We cannot take the risk of letting a serpent roam around the house. We have a baby, after all, and I'm worried that the wily snake will cause harm. I will continue searching for him under the heaps of pots, where it is cooler, I'm sure he finds it comfortable to stay there and hide.'

Suddenly, Champa noticed a mouse sitting in a corner of the house. The mouse whispered, 'These people don't know that the serpent comes to eat me. But I am smarter than the snake, so I go and hide under one of the pots in a tiny hole. The serpent looks for me everywhere and breaks many pots. Anyway, I come to this potter's house only to find four grains of rice to eat. If I get that from elsewhere, I won't ever need to go to the potter's house again.'

Hearing that, Champa turned and ran inside her house. She brought a handful of rice and gave it to Mini. In her mind, she spoke to the mouse sitting in the potter's house, 'I am giving some rice to Mini. She will give this to you. Eat four grains a day, but don't trouble anyone any more. When the rice is finished, tell Mini and I will send you more.'

The mouse was very happy and thanked Champa. Mini ran off to give the rice to the mouse.

The serpent never saw the mouse after that, and so, he stopped going to the potter's house. He went to another forest in search of another mouse. The potter was happy that his pots and his family were safe. The elephant, too, was happy to be left alone now that the serpent was gone. He thanked the lord of the lake and promised not to trouble him any more. The lord was happy and sent a message to the parrot, 'Your family has been our companion for generations, so come back. Just don't make your home on the branch that nearly touches the water. Instead, do it a little higher so that we can all coexist and live together.'

The bird thanked the queen and decided to go back home to the tree. The queen wanted to give the parrot some jewellery, but he refused. 'No, I don't need jewels. You have taken care of me all these days and I have enjoyed my stay. I will take memories of our time together home with me. Goodbye. I will go now,' he said, and flew away.

With the bird's departure, the queen had a lot of time to spare. She realized that she hadn't opened the door at the top of the palace for a long time, which the king had been asking her to do for a while now. She opened the door and a strong gust of wind came through and pushed the clouds. The clouds floated away and the sun started shining brightly. The grass below got plenty of sunshine and soon became dry, as did the wood sitting on it.

Champa's mother came out of the house soon after and saw Champa standing in the backyard, doing nothing. She nudged her, 'Hey Champa, I asked you to bring firewood. What are you doing here? Daydreaming?'

'Mother, you don't know where I have been! Do you know that four grains of rice can change the world? Please give me a handful of rice every week. My Mini should not suffer like the others.'

Champa's mother had no idea what her daughter was talking about, but like a mother does, she smiled and gave her a handful of rice.

The Mouse That Became a Mouse

The night was pitch dark and the children were sitting on the steps near the veranda. There was a coolness in the air, despite the summer setting in.

Suddenly, Aditi yelled, 'Are those fireflies? See how they twinkle and disappear!'

Ajji lit a lamp nearby. 'The light from the matchstick is stronger,' she said.

'But a candle's is even stronger, Ajji!' said Krishna.

Raghu flashed the torch on his mobile phone. 'Now that is more powerful than a candle,' said Meenu.

'Every light does its own duty,' said Ajji. 'You can't enjoy the firefly during the day, and the same goes for moonlight. Every source of light has its own glow and purpose. Come, I will tell you a story about who is

69

most powerful. Remember, you are your own person and you are powerful exactly the way you are.'

Anoushka looked at her, confused.

'Tell me,' Ajji asked her. 'Which light do you enjoy the most—the one from a firefly, a matchstick, a candle or a torch?'

'The firefly, of course,' said Anoushka. The others nodded their heads in agreement.

'Why?'

'Because it is natural and fascinating, Ajji,' said Meenu.

Ajji smiled.

Once upon a time, there lived a sage in an ashram in the Himalayas. One day, while he was meditating, he heard someone running towards him. The noise disturbed his concentration and he opened his eyes to see a mouse sweating heavily and trembling with fear. The sage was compassionate. 'What happened, little mouse? Why are you scared?' he asked.

'Sir, I've come to your ashram as I have heard of your great yogic powers. I am being chased by my eternal enemy, the cat.'

'Don't worry, you will be safe here,' assured the sage.

'But I can't stay here forever. Will you do me a favour?'

'Tell me, mouse.'

'Please turn me into a cat. Then I won't be scared of them and will lead a happy life.'

The sage smiled. 'That is not true, but I will fulfil your desire.'

He blessed the mouse, and the mouse-turned-cat happily ran away.

A few uneventful days passed. But then again, one day, the sage heard a noise that interrupted his meditation. When he opened his eyes, he saw that it was the same mouse-cat, sweating heavily and trembling with fear.

'What is the matter?' asked the sage.

'Sir, I enjoyed my days as a cat for some time. But now, I am scared of the dog that chases me around. I didn't know that dogs hated cats.'

'What do you want?'

'Please turn me into a dog. Then I won't be scared of dogs and will lead a happy life.'

The sage smiled. 'That is not true, but I will fulfil your desire.'

The cat now turned into a dog and happily ran away.

Some more days passed before the sage heard someone running towards him again, breaking his meditation. He opened his eyes to see the mouse-cat-dog sweating heavily and trembling with fear.

'What is the matter?' asked the sage.

'There is an animal called the lion—he is the king of the forest. He is huge and powerful. When he roars, everybody gets scared. He can eat anyone and I am only a small animal, after all,' said the dog.

'What do you want?'

'Please turn me into a lion. Then I will rule the forest and will lead a happy life.'

The sage smiled. 'That is not true, but I will fulfil your desire.'

The dog then turned into a roaring lion and happily ran away.

This time, months passed before the sage heard the familiar sound of someone running towards him. He stopped meditating and opened his eyes.

The same mouse-cat-dog-lion stood before him, sweating heavily and itching all over.

'What is the matter?' asked the sage.

'I have enjoyed my reign in the forest for some time. It was wonderful. Recently, though, there are small insects called ants entering my skin and my ears. If they'd been big animals, I would have killed them instantly, but these ants are so small that I can't even see them. The itching on my body and ears is unbearable,' said the lion.

'What do you want?'

'Please turn me into an ant and I will lead a happy life.'

The sage smiled. 'That is not true, but I will fulfil your desire.'

The lion promptly turned into an ant and happily scurried away.

Weeks passed before, once again, the sage heard someone running towards him. He paused his meditation and opened his eyes.

It was the same mouse-cat-dog-lion-ant, limping.

'What is the matter?' asked the sage.

'Do you remember me, sir? I am the mouse-cat-dog-lion-ant. I had a good but an extremely hard-working life. We worked in teams and I loved it. We built a beautiful castle for ourselves, but one day, a reptile known as a snake came and took over our home. We took many months to build the house and he came and occupied it as if it was his own. What an insensitive fellow! We couldn't fight him because he was huge.

While leaving, he pushed me aside and that is why I am limping,' said the ant.

'What do you want?'

'Please turn me into a snake, the most powerful reptile. Then I will lead a happy life.'

The sage smiled. 'That is not true, but I will fulfil your desire.'

The ant turned into a hissing snake and happily slithered away.

A few more weeks passed. Then again, the sage heard someone running towards him while he was meditating. He opened his eyes.

Badly injured, the same mouse-cat-dog-lion-ant-snake had come again.

'What is the matter?' asked the sage.

'It is a long story,' said the snake. 'I went to a godown to catch a mouse. Mice are very delicious meals. But the godown owner tried to hit me even though I hadn't harmed him. So I hissed at him in anger, but he hit me more and injured me. See the wounds on my body! That's why I ran away and came here.'

'What do you want?'

'Please turn me into a man, who can beat even the most powerful reptile. Then I will lead a happy life.'

The sage smiled. 'That is not true, but I will fulfil your desire.'

The snake then turned into a young man and happily went his way.

Several months passed before the sage heard the sound of someone running towards him again. The noise interrupted his meditation, and he opened his eyes.

It was the same mouse-cat-dog-lion-ant-snake-man.

'What is the matter?' asked the sage.

'Swamiji, I am really tired. Every day, I worked hard and stored grains for a rainy day. But a small mouse came and made holes in the bags of grains, and started to take them away bit by bit. We didn't even notice it at first! Then snakes began entering our storage area in search of mice, and they terrify me,' said the young man.

'What do you want?'

'Turn me back into a mouse, who can hide inside the hole without anyone noticing me. Then I will lead a happy life.'

The sage smiled. 'That is not true, but I will fulfil your desire.'

The young man turned into a mouse and scurried away.

Some more time passed. One day, once again, the sage heard someone running towards him as he meditated. He stopped and opened his eyes.

It was the same mouse-cat-dog-lion-ant-snake-man-mouse.

The sage smiled and said, 'You may always wish to run back to me, child. Life is an experience. We all face challenges on this journey. If you are beautiful, there will be a person more beautiful than you. If you are brave, there will be a person braver than you. If you are witty, there will be a person who is wittier than you. Accept what has been given to you. I knew you would be back since the day you asked me to change you into a cat, but I allowed you to have this experience and learn from it! I bless you — may you avoid your enemies and lead a good life,' blessed the sage.

The mouse nodded as understanding dawned on him, and he left the ashram with happiness and a twinkle in his eyes.

Forty Days of Quarantine

The next day, Ajja and Ajji were talking to each other over their morning tea. 'We cannot entertain the children like we did the last time they were here,' said Ajja, 'since we cannot go out at all. We can't take them to the local market or to a wedding or to a picnic or even Rehmat's house. Though the atmosphere is not a happy one, we have to do our best to keep their spirits up. Let's try and distract the children as much as we can.'

Ajji nodded and added, 'The children must not forget their schoolwork either, so I want to create a routine and a daily timetable for them. Every morning, they must get up early and finish their chores. They can sit down to study after breakfast.'

'I like the idea,' agreed Ajja. 'Let me take charge. We will tell them to study well until lunch. We can tell them stories in the afternoons and they can play in the garden in the evenings.'

'How about we teach them the traditional games that we played at home when we were young? Remember playing hopscotch, snakes and ladders, Scrabble and ludo?' asked Ajji, excited. 'I think it will help keep the children happy and engaged. They can help in some of the work with the distribution of food too!'

Kamlu Ajji sighed, 'Thank God they are here. We have also been feeling better by having them around. Otherwise, we would have been terribly bored and lonely.'

Soon, Ajja made a timetable and called out to the children. They came running, and happily agreed to follow the schedule.

Aditi asked, 'Ajja, has this kind of lockdown and isolation ever happened before? Have you experienced anything like this when you were young?'

'That's an excellent question, Aditi! I was only a year old when the Second World War happened. I don't remember anything, of course. My mother told me that there was a tight ration and food supply. Travel was also limited then, but the population of our country was smaller too. In my adult life, we faced many power cuts during the war with China in 1962. That's when I learnt to preserve electricity and not waste it.'

Ajji chuckled, 'That's why Ajja switches off the light whenever we leave a room. It's a habit that has stayed with him since then.'

'But I have never faced anything like this, children. My grandmother used to tell me about the plague, the cholera and even the Spanish flu. Villages were evacuated and people were forced to move elsewhere to find a place to stay, but we did and can conquer anything as a human race. For now, we must understand and obey the rules of social distancing and quarantine.'

'What is the meaning of quarantine?' Anoushka asked.

'It means a period of isolation, originally forty days—as per its origin in Latin and Italian,' said Ajji.

'Do you know a story about quarantine?'

Ajji smiled.

'Tell us a story, Ajji!' shouted the children, excited.

Anmol was an orphan who worked in a restaurant to earn money. He would work all day and take leftover food back to his small hut, which stood near a river. He would sit by the river with his food, and feed the fishes in the water.

Months passed. Anmol was not making enough money to improve his standard of life and wondered how he could earn some more so that he could save for a rainy day.

One day, a stranger passing through the village ate lunch at the restaurant where Anmol worked. From his appearance, the stranger looked like a rich man.

Anmol waited on him and the stranger began talking to him. 'Hi, I am Deepak,' he said.

'What brings you here?' asked Anmol. 'There is nothing special about this village and we rarely get travellers.'

Deepak said, 'I am a successful merchant and need an assistant to help with my business. My terms and conditions are simple. I want a young and active boy. For the first forty days, I will not ask him to do any work. In fact, he will be fed well and taken care of. Then he will have to work for only two hours for which I will give him a gold coin in advance, and nine more after the work is done. I am in search of a dependable person who would agree to my terms. So, I will be here for a few days.'

Since the village was mostly filled with pensioners, Anmol was one of the few people eligible for the job. After Deepak left, Anmol thought to himself, *If I get ten gold coins, I can buy a property here. Perhaps this will allow me to live a better life.*

The next day, Anmol approached Deepak and said, 'Sir, I am willing to work for you.'

Deepak was happy and took Anmol back to the city, gave him a nice room and said that he would take care of him for forty days, but that Anmol couldn't go out without him. He had to remain cut off from the rest of the world. Deepak was true to his word and Anmol got good food every day, he got to go to different places in the city, accompanied by Deepak, and felt as though he was on a wonderful holiday.

Once the forty days were over, Deepak said, 'You can go home after completing two hours of work tomorrow. Here is one gold coin for you, and the rest I will give you after the work is done.'

The next morning, Deepak and Anmol set out on a journey into a deep forest. Deepak carried an enormous empty leather bag with him. Soon, the duo approached a steep hill that ended in a cliff with a strong river flowing below.

Deepak stopped walking. He turned to Anmol and said, 'I want to gather some fruits from the forest and take them home, but I don't know how much weight the bag can hold. Will you climb into the bag? I will lift it up with you inside it so that I can get an estimate of how much weight it can hold.'

'Of course,' said Anmol.

The moment he was inside the bag, Deepak locked it. Only his head could be seen outside the bag.

Anmol didn't understand what was happening. Shocked and scared, he shrieked, 'What are you doing?'

Without saying a word, Deepak wrapped the bag in meat. A few minutes later, a huge eagle swooped down and carried the bag to the top of the hill.

Once the eagle had reached the top, it began unintentionally opening the knots on the bag in an effort to eat as much meat as possible. Quickly, Anmol managed to come out of one end of the bag.

Deepak was standing at the foot of the hill and Anmol could see him.

Deepak shouted, 'Don't be afraid. There is a lot of treasure around you. Please start throwing down as much as you can.'

'But, sir, this eagle will eat me after it finishes eating the meat!'

'Don't worry, there is another way to come down from the hill. Finish the task quickly,' instructed Deepak. The eagle was still eating and pecking at the meat aggressively.

Once he had thrown some of the treasure down the hill, Anmol shouted, 'Enough. I want to get off this hill. Tell me how!'

'You foolish boy, can't you see the skeletons and empty bags around you? Most of the men stayed back and got eaten by the eagle. The only way to get out of there is to jump off the cliff, into the river. Good luck with your decision! It's time for me to go,' sniggered Deepak as he quickly finished collecting the treasure and walked away.

Anmol became deathly afraid. He understood why Deepak had put him in what was surely forty days of quarantine—it was so that enough time passes to make sure that nobody came looking for him in case he went missing. Now, Anmol had two choices—die at the hands of the eagle or jump off the cliff into the river below.

Anmol thought, *It is better to jump and die at once rather than suffer for a long time by being pecked at by the eagle.*

He jumped, hopeless in the face of the fate that awaited him. Little did he know, it was the same river that later passed through his village, near his hut, and was inhabited by the same fishes he used to feed every day. When he fell down and began to sink, one of the fishes recognized him and dragged a small wooden log to him. Anmol clung to it, and thanked the fish as they guided him and followed the river moving upstream until he reached the riverbank near his hut.

He went home, aghast at the trick Deepak had played.

After a few days, Anmol heard that Deepak was visiting a neighbouring village looking for a new recruit.

One of Anmol's friends wanted to jump on the offer, but he alerted him. 'I have one gold coin. I will give it to you, but please don't go. It is dangerous.'

He managed to convince his friend and saved his life.

He travelled to the neighbouring village and approached Deepak. When Deepak noticed him, he stared at him in disbelief.

'Sir, I have come to collect the rest of my payment,' demanded Anmol.

'But . . . but . . . how did you come down from the hill?' asked Deepak, as he counted nine gold coins and gave them to Anmol.

'I found a tunnel a little distance from where the eagle had dropped me and ran out. It brought me to the bottom of the hill. There is still a lot of jewellery and treasure left there. Sir, you can go and pick up whatever you want since you are a better judge when it comes to choosing the more expensive treasures. But you need to apply more meat to the bag to keep the eagle busy for a longer time.'

Deepak thought about it and decided to go to the cliff himself. He asked Anmol, 'Will you come with me? I'll pay you.'

'Sure, I'll come with you. But I don't need any more payment. The ten gold coins are enough. I am happy as I am,' said Anmol.

The next morning, Deepak and Anmol walked to the forest. When they reached the hill, Deepak climbed into the bag and the huge eagle picked it up and flew to the top of the hill.

Once he was there, Deepak was surprised to see the exquisite jewels glinting in the sun. He didn't know which ones to pick and which ones to leave.

'I will throw you lots of jewels. Please collect them and keep them safe,' he shouted to Anmol, who was standing below.

Deepak threw down the jewels until the eagle had finished the meat on the bag and began to approach him. 'Anmol,' Deepak called out, 'tell me how to escape.'

'Sir, the only way to get out of there is to jump off the cliff, into the river. Good luck with your decision! It's time for me to go,' said Anmol, as he quickly finished collecting the jewels and walked away.

Deepak jumped into the water. The fish, however, did not recognize him. With no one to help him, Deepak drowned.

What's Luck Got to Do with It?

Just as the grandparents had planned, Ajja began teaching the children every day. He was the headmaster of his five-student school.

His methodology was different from the teachers in the children's schools. Ajja always introduced topics and tied them to a story.

Raghu asked, 'Ajja, why do you teach everything through a story?'

'A long, long time ago, stories were used to teach various subjects and life skills. The thought was that children will find things easier to understand if concepts are explained through interesting stories or anecdotes. People say that there once lived a king whose sons refused to listen to their teachers. A courtier suggested,

"Sire, you can send your children to the forest to live with a teacher I know. Then they will be forced to pay attention and get an education." The king liked the idea and sent his sons to the teacher who lived in the forest. There, the teacher taught the boys about everything in life using animals and analogies, always in the form of a story—that is the origin of the Panchatantra. Eventually, the king's sons became responsible and mature and the king was filled with gratitude towards the teacher.'

'I know the Panchatantra!' piped in Anoushka.

The children laughed.

Ajja nodded and continued, 'That is why, traditionally, in India, stories were often used to teach lessons—it could be a moral, a mathematical concept or about administration. The Panchatantra was made for teaching children. The Indian mathematician Bhaskara's text, called *Lilavati*, elaborated on the subject by telling stories and included even the Pythagoras' theorem. In the west, lessons were taken strictly as lessons only and they would often tell stories only during bedtime. In time, teaching with data and statistics became the tools of formal teaching. Today, stories are meant for entertainment, but I belong to the old school of thought. In my younger days, I used to be a schoolteacher. Even today, when you meet my students, ask them what they remember about me. Most will say, "The stories that taught us lessons."'

'Ajja, are your students successful? Did listening to the stories help them?' asked Meenu.

Ajja chuckled. 'Some have. But to achieve success, you need hard work, determination and a dab of luck. Luck doesn't knock on your door all the time. But when it does, you must be ready for it. Now, that reminds me of Ravi.'

'Who is Ravi?'

'He is a man who received gold due to luck, but also realized that it was not the way to live,' replied Ajja.

'Tell us more, Ajja!' Anoushka begged.

'I will, once you finish all your work with focus and without keeping anything pending for tomorrow.'

The incentive brought back the children's attention to their studies and they completed their schoolwork with speed and accuracy.

After they had all finished, Ajja began the story.

Ravi was a simple man and a self-sufficient farmer. Farming, however, depends a lot on rain and doesn't always fetch enough money. His wife, Alka, was unhappy about the fact. She would often compare herself to others and say, 'Oh! My husband doesn't earn much. I am so unlucky.'

One day, Alka went to the market to buy vegetables. At a vendor's cart, she saw a lady approaching the vendor, her assistant in tow. Alka stared at the woman's jewellery and her fine silk sari. The vegetable vendor didn't even care to speak to Alka, he attended to the rich lady first. After she left, Alka asked the vendor, 'Who is she?'

'Don't you know? She is the wife of the royal astrologer who predicts the future and finds missing things in the king's court,' said the vendor.

Alka came home, fuming. She turned to her husband, frustrated. 'Look at my life. Even the vegetable vendor doesn't respect me, even though I am a regular customer. I think you should become an astrologer.'

'How can I? I don't know anything about astrology,' said Ravi.

'There's nothing to it. Roll the dice and say whatever comes to your mind,' said Alka and kept insisting that he try it.

After a few days, a helpless Ravi agreed. Dressed as an astrologer, he carried a dice and sat near the crossroads in the market. Nobody looked in his direction or approached him. After a few hours, a lady came and said, 'Sir, my husband gave me a precious ring, but I have forgotten where I kept it. If I don't find it, I will be in trouble. Please help me locate the ring.'

Ravi started to sweat. He didn't know what to do or what to say. He cast the dice and a number came up. Suddenly, he thought that the dice also looked like a small matchbox. He said to himself, 'It looks like a matchbox!'

As soon as the lady heard him mutter those words, she turned around and ran home.

After an hour, she came back and gave him a gold coin. 'What a prediction you made!' she said. 'I placed the ring in a matchbox and completely forgot about it! I went home and found it. Thank you very much!'

Ravi took the coin and went home. Alka was ecstatic. 'I told you so, didn't I? You wouldn't have earned a gold coin even if you had farmed our land for a full year!'

'It was simply a matter of chance,' said Ravi. 'I said something absent-mindedly while looking at the dice, but she mistook the words for a prediction and found what she was looking for. Alka, I'd rather work in the fields where I know what I am doing. I do not want to go sit in the market tomorrow.'

Alka, however, was stubborn. She didn't listen to her husband and forced him to agree to go to the market again the next day.

Meanwhile, that very night, forty boxes of jewels were stolen from the palace. The king was furious. He called the royal astrologer and ordered him, 'Find out who has taken the treasure and where it is! I want an immediate answer!'

The royal astrologer couldn't come up with any details and informed a minister about his inability to find out who the robber was.

When the king was informed about this, a courtier stood up and said, 'Sire, my wife met an astrologer near the market crossroads. She praised him greatly, it seems he is very good.' The king summoned Ravi to his court immediately.

'Yesterday, forty boxes of jewels got stolen from the treasury. Tell me who has them and when I will get them back. If you don't provide the right information, I will throw you in jail indefinitely,' the king commanded Ravi.

Ravi began to sweat with nervousness and cursed Alka quietly. He had never imagined he'd be caught in such a dangerous scenario. He cast the dice and pretended to calculate something in his mind.

The king demanded, 'Tell me now, where are the forty boxes?'

Ravi heard forty and mumbled, 'Forty people.'

'What?'

'Your boxes were taken by forty people,' said Ravi, committing to what he had said earlier.

'The royal astrologer couldn't even figure out that much. Which direction are these thieves headed?'

'I need forty days,' said Ravi, knowing that saying anything more could land him in jail.

'I don't have so much time.'

'I require forty days, sire,' said Ravi. 'That's what is being said to me. I can't help it.'

'Fine, come back to me with the forty boxes or you will find yourself in jail for life.'

Ravi went back home. Scared to death, he told Alka what had happened. Alka felt terribly sorry. 'Oh my God, my greed and ego are the cause of all your troubles. If you go to jail, it will be my fault,' she cried.

She wept and sobbed and tried to think of a solution, but she couldn't see a way out.

Ravi was in a sombre mood. He took his favourite treat from the storeroom—dates. He counted forty and put them in a box. 'Alka,' he said with sadness in his heart. 'If I have to go to jail in forty days, I want to enjoy a date each day before that happens. After forty days, I will go back to the king's court to face the consequences.'

The truth was, in fact, that there were forty thieves, who each took one box of jewels from the king's treasury. The news of the new astrologer reached them through their spy in the king's court.

The leader of the thieves said, 'Don't worry, my men. I don't think this Ravi can trace us. But to be safe, let's hold on to the treasure for forty days. Moving it around at this time increases the risk of us getting caught.'

The men, however, were worried.

'Sir, I will go and investigate Ravi's plans today,' one of the thieves announced. The leader gave him permission to do so.

The man climbed to the terrace of Ravi's house. Before he could peep inside, he heard a voice, 'You have forty days, dear husband. Wait until then.'

Ravi replied.

'What did you say?' asked Alka.

Ravi ate a date and sighed. He said, 'One is finished. Thirty-nine are left.'

Without waiting to hear more, the thief ran away.

He came and reported back to the leader, 'Sir, I climbed the terrace on the astrologer's house and he said—one is finished, thirty-nine are left. He knew I was there, so I ran away!'

The leader was curious. He said, 'Okay, two of you must go to his house tomorrow.'

Meanwhile, Alka was miserable at the situation her husband was in. He had neither the knowledge of astrology nor any power. She felt sorry that she had pushed her husband to pretend to be an astrologer and apologized to him several times. 'Perhaps I should go and tell the king the truth,' she suggested.

'Even if you do, no one will believe you. People really think that I am an established astrologer. Alka, life would have been so much better and happier if we had just kept a low profile and led a free life as farmers.'

Alka sobbed bitterly.

The two men climbed to the terrace of Ravi's house. Before they could peep inside, they heard a man's voice say, 'Two are finished. Thirty-eight are left.' Ravi had eaten the second date.

Without waiting to hear more, the thieves ran away.

They came and reported to the leader, 'Sir, we climbed to the terrace of the astrologer's house and he said, "Two are finished, thirty-eight are left." He knew we were there, so we ran away.'

The leader was curious. He said, 'Okay, three of you must go to his house tomorrow.'

This continued until the fortieth day, when the leader also went to Ravi's house.

All the men went to Ravi's house. Before they could peep inside, they heard a man's voice say, 'All forty are finished, Alka, and now there is no escape.'

'What did you say?' asked Alka.

'Done. They are finished. I will go to the king's court right now and report back,' he said.

Seconds later, there was a knock on the door.

'I know why you have come,' said Ravi, thinking that the king's guards had arrived to escort him to the king or the jail.

When he opened the door, the leader of the thieves fell down at his feet and said, 'Please save us. We are thieves, not murderers. If the king learns that we are responsible for the robbery, he will hang us.'

'Do you have all the treasure?' asked Ravi, trying to hide his astonishment.

'Yes, sir, we have the forty boxes. Once we heard about you and the waiting period of forty days, we decided to wait and see.'

'In that case, keep all the boxes under the big banyan tree on the outskirts of my village and go back into hiding. I will take care of the rest,' said Ravi.

The leader agreed, relieved.

The next day, Ravi sent word to the king. The note read: 'Sire, I have found information about the treasure, but due to the limitations of my powers, I can only give you one bit of information—either the location of the treasure or the location of the thieves. What would you like to choose?'

Even though he had sent a note, Ravi was terrified. Though logic dictated that the king would be inclined to choose the location of the treasure, Ravi wondered what he would do if the king decided to choose the location of the thieves instead.

He spent the day in suspense.

A day later, the king sent his reply. 'I want the treasure,' said the note.

Ravi thanked his stars and sent back another note, 'I have located the treasure and used my powers to transport the boxes under the ground of the big banyan tree on the outskirts of my village.'

The king sent his soldiers and after a little digging, they found the forty boxes of treasure. Nothing was missing.

The king was pleased and invited Ravi to his court. There, the king said, 'I want to offer you the position of the royal astrologer. You can start today.'

Ravi knew that he must not fall into this trap again. He said, 'No, sire, I have spent all my energy and days tracing these forty boxes of treasure. My power has diminished to a great extent and I will not be able to predict anything in the future. I am not fit to be a royal astrologer now.'

The king nodded. He felt sorry for Ravi and said, 'I will never meet someone like you ever again, so I would like to present you with one box of the treasure as a gift.'

Ravi thanked him and left the court as quickly as possible. Alka and Ravi lived a content and peaceful life for the rest of their days.

'Aaah, what a story!' exclaimed Kamlu Ajji, who had joined them quietly and was sitting nearby, sorting oranges. 'You tell a nice tale, brother!'

Ajja grinned. 'Well, you must also tell a story.'

'Oh no, not now. I am busy trying to count the number of oranges needed for a glass of orange juice. How many children are there? Five, right?' she mumbled to herself.

'Please, Kamlu,' said Ajja. 'Let the children hear another story.'

'Okay, but then lunch will be delayed by fifteen minutes.'

'We don't mind, Ajji,' said Anoushka, who was the youngest and always ready for a story.

'Fine, but I must remind you to follow the rules during this time. What are the rules, children?'

'Wash hands frequently,' said Raghu.

'In case of a runny nose, a cough or if we are feeling feverish, we must report to one of the grandparents,' said Meenu.

'Keep a minimum distance of five feet at all times as much as possible,' said Krishna.

'We are all not allowed to go beyond the wall of the compound,' said Aditi.

'We should not touch our eyes, mouth and nose unnecessarily,' said Anoushka.

'Excellent,' said Kamlu Ajji, and then started telling them the story.

Raghava was a simple young boy who lived alone. He didn't have a family or anyone to advise him. He was often fooled by people smarter than him. People called him for work but didn't pay him properly at the end of it, or paid him less than the agreed amount. Poor Raghava kept quiet because he didn't know how to negotiate with them or even confront them.

Because of his innocent nature, he came to be known as Bhola Raghava.

He became tired of his endless poverty. No matter what he did, he always ended up tricked or cheated.

One day, a sage consoled him by saying, 'When luck is on one's side, a simple action can change one's destiny. Wait, my young friend. Your time will come!'

A few days later, Raghava was sitting under a tree when he heard two people talking loudly to each other, a short distance away. One of them said, 'You never know. An act of God can change anyone's life, but it's important that God be happy with you.'

Tired of his poverty, Raghava interrupted their conversation, 'But how will I know if God is happy with me unless I meet him?'

The duo looked at Raghava and one of them said, 'If you pray with love and sincerity, God is sure to see you and bless you.'

Raghava had only one companion—his loyal horse. The two were inseparable. So Raghava rode his horse to the forest and sat down on a rock. He prayed sincerely, 'I am honest, and I try to work hard. I need your help. Please come and bless me.' Within hours, he heard a voice in his ears, 'Get up, child. Go and sleep. When morning comes, with your eyes closed, extend your hands and touch something around you when you wake up. It will change your life.'

Raghava knew that the voice was special and went back home on his horse. He had a few coins with him and he kept them next to him when he slept that night. He thought that if he touched them in the morning, they may multiply and change his life.

In the early hours of the morning, a cat entered Raghava's house and the horse suddenly became restless. Raghava heard the horse's neighing, woke up and with his eyes closed, reached the horse and touched his bell as he opened his eyes fully.

Raghava shook his head when he realized what he had done. The coins were right next to his bed, untouched. He laughed at himself and thought, *My love for the horse has probably cost me a better life. How can this bell change my life?*

Pushing the thoughts aside, Raghava took the horse and decided to go to the city, which was some distance away.

It was noon and before long, he felt hot and decided to take a break under a shady banyan tree. There, he saw a young mother and her baby. The baby was crying uncontrollably and nobody around could help soothe the baby. A few minutes later, the mother gave up and began to cry too.

Raghava decided to leave and as soon as the horse took a few steps, the bell began to ring and the baby stopped crying. So Raghava rang the bell for a while, till the baby was completely calm. The mother was relieved and said, 'At last! My child is happy now because of the sound of the bell. Oh young man, will you give this old bell to me? In return, I will give you five juicy oranges. Unfortunately, that is all that I can give you.'

Compassionate Raghava exchanged the bell for the oranges.

When he reached the next village, he passed by a big house. A big crowd was standing outside.

'What is the matter?' he asked a girl standing in front of the house.

'Our mother is very sick. The doctor says that she must have very juicy fruits immediately so that she can survive. We don't have any such fruits nearby and we need some right now,' said the beautiful young girl, who looked like she was about to cry any moment now.

Raghava felt sorry for her and gave her the five oranges. 'Here, I have some. Take these. Maybe it can be of some use to your mother,' he said gently.

The girl ran inside and he decided to wait for a few minutes to see how her mother was doing. After some time, the girl came out of the house looking for him.

She said, 'Mother is feeling better. You have saved her life! She has sent this gift for you.'

The girl gave him a fine silk scarf, thanked him and ran back into the house.

Raghava went further towards the city. After some time, he took a break and had lunch with a group of travellers who offered to share food with him. One of them said, 'We really like your scarf. The quality is wonderful. I have a fine dagger and I can give that to you in exchange for the scarf. Tell me, will you make this exchange?'

Raghava agreed to take the dagger in exchange for the scarf.

By the time he reached the main market of the city, it was evening. There was a big commotion. Someone told him that the king was coming and everyone was waiting for him.

When the king arrived, everyone stood still—almost like dolls.

Raghava was fascinated by the king's grandeur.

The king's eye fell on Raghava and the dagger that he had kept tied around his midriff. The king asked, 'Young lad, your dagger has caught my fancy. You are not a warrior, but I am. This dagger is exactly what I need. Will you give it to me?'

'Please take it, sire!' said Raghava immediately.

In return, the king gave him a lot of money.

Raghava used the coins to find a room to rest in an inn and a stable for his horse. At dinner, he heard a merchant say to a friend, 'I desperately need some funds. The material I had ordered is coming early tomorrow morning and I need to pay for the delivery. If someone loans me money just for a day, I can pay them back double tomorrow once I sell all the wares. But it is night already. Who can help me at such short notice?'

Raghava turned around and said to the merchant, 'I can help. I can give the money you need. You can pay me back the same amount tomorrow.'

The merchant was surprised that a young lad was going to help him without any conditions. So the merchant said, 'Thank you for the generous offer.

Whatever I get, I will give you half of it. Please wait at the inn until I am back tomorrow.'

The next evening, Raghava waited for the merchant, who came back and said to him, 'Oh lad, you have brought me luck. The money you gave me has doubled, like I thought it would, but to my surprise, it has doubled in gold coins because the princess herself has bought all my material.'

The merchant handed over a big bag of gold coins to Raghava and invited him to be his partner. The merchant considered Raghava to be his lucky charm.

Raghava agreed and soon enough, he became a very rich man. He made a nice stable for his horse and took good care of him.

Many marriage proposals started pouring in.

One day, Raghava saw a young girl at the market; she was the same girl whose mother had given him a silk scarf. He approached her and asked, 'How is your mother?'

'Oh! It is so nice to see you here! I cannot forget what you did for my family. We tried to trace you but failed,' she said.

Raghava smiled and gave her his address.

That evening, he received another marriage proposal and to his pleasant surprise, it was from the family of the girl he had met at the market.

When night fell, Raghava took his horse for a ride and said to him, 'When luck is on one's side, a simple bell can change one's destiny. Thank you for being my loyal companion on this journey.'

The next day, Raghava agreed to the proposal, and the two were wed and lived a happy life together.

'That is why I pray in the temple before my exam results. I believe that God always blesses us with luck, so I request him to send me some whenever I need it,' said Raghu.

'Me too!' said Krishna.

Kamlu Ajji laughed and left to make lunch.

A Word of Honour

Two days later, there was a call from a town officer in the morning.

When Ajja picked up the phone, the officer requested him to put him on speaker so that he could speak to both Ajja and Ajji.

Then he said, 'A few construction workers have landed here. Since there were no buses, trains or flights, these group of workers began making their way home from Hubli. On the way, these migrant workers realized that they could not reach their homes in the north, but they have managed to reach our town on their way. As we are in quarantine, I have arranged for them to stay at the Hanuman temple in the outskirts. There are a few taps there, along with some public toilets. I told them to stay put until the lockdown is over and they can reach home safely. They have agreed to do so, but we need to send them food every day. Once they are settled in, perhaps in three to four days, we can give them gas and dry ration so that they can start cooking themselves. But right now, they are not in a position to make food themselves.'

'How many people are there?' asked Ajja.

'Around twenty-five men. Is there any way you can send something to eat from your house for today's lunch?'

Immediately, Ajja said, 'Of course, we will send chapatis for them.'

Ajji nodded in agreement.

'That's an excellent idea,' said the town officer. 'I am sure that they will like chapatis. Meanwhile, I will ask someone else for cooked vegetables.'

Ajji, who was always ready to help, jumped in and said, 'Don't worry. We will cook some vegetables too. Let us know what we should cook each day.'

The town officer sounded relieved and happy. 'Thank you for your donation. May your tribe increase! I will keep you updated.'

Ajji went to the storeroom and exclaimed, 'Oh no! We don't have enough wheat flour to feed twenty-five people.'

Kamlu Ajji agreed, 'I think this will make only fifty chapatis. We have wheat at home, but it needs to be ground into flour. The grinding machine shop will open for only an hour in the evening due to the lockdown. And remember, we have to feed the children also. If we add Damu and us, we will still need around thirty more chapatis. What should we do?'

'There's no question about it! I have given my word of honour. I must send the workers one hundred chapatis.'

Ajji glanced at the clock. It was 10 a.m. The grocery store opened for three hours between 6 and 9 p.m.

'I can call the town officer and tell him that we will give them the chapatis tomorrow. We can just get the groceries today,' suggested Ajja.

'Perhaps we can eat rice today and somehow make one hundred chapatis to send to the men. But how?' The children were surprised to see that Ajji was very anxious and worried. Usually, she was calm and happy all the time, but she had become tense when she found out that the flour they had was insufficient.

Suddenly, Ajji thought of checking with Damu, who was drinking a cup of tea and listening to the conversation.

'Do you have wheat flour at home, Damu?'

'Yes, Amma. I can get it. It should be enough.'

'Okay then, I'll get you the flour in the evening and replace it.'

Damu ran to get the flour from the house next door.

Relieved, Ajji went to the kitchen to start preparing the dough.

Kamlu Ajji went to the garden to pluck fresh leafy vegetables. They were easy to grow, unlike other vegetables. Ajji shouted out to the children, 'Raghu, Meenu, go and bring me drumsticks from the tree.

Drumsticks are nutritious and easy to make if one has lesser time at hand.'

Raghu and Meenu ran to the garden to do her bidding.

After a few minutes, Anoushka, Aditi and Krishna went to the kitchen. Anoushka asked, 'Ajji, why were you so stressed when you found out that we didn't have enough flour? You could have given the chapatis tomorrow, right?'

'No, child. I had given my word of honour. Perhaps I should have checked how much flour we had and then committed to providing so many chapatis to the town officer.'

'*Word of honour*—why is it so important, Ajji?'

'Once you say that you will do something, you must complete it. Sometimes, it is easy to come up with genuine reasons to not do what you have committed to, but that is not right. A person is known to be dependable only if he or she does what they have said without excuses or reasons.'

'Like military rule,' said Krishna.

'That is why soldiers are dependable people,' replied Ajji, as Ajja entered the kitchen.

'We live safely in democratic India because they are there for us, reliably guarding our borders,' added Ajja.

Ajji smiled.

'What happened, Ajji?' asked Aditi.

'Talking to you girls about this reminded me of a story.'

'Please tell us, Ajji,' insisted Aditi.

'Sure, I will tell you while making the chapatis.'

King Narendra was the ruler of a small kingdom. He was well known because he was a king who was always true to his word of honour.

One year, the kingdom faced a heavy drought. The king announced, 'There will be no celebrations or luxurious food in the court or the palace. I will eat whatever my subjects eat, till the drought has ended.'

The king opened his kitchen to everyone— something a king had never done before. This endeared him to his subjects. True to his word, this continued until the rains arrived and the drought ended.

A few months later, the king began to build a palace on an enormous piece of land. A very old and worn-out hut stood next to this land.

The person who lived in the hut approached the king and said, 'Sire, someone is building a really big house next to my land. People are asking me to vacate my home to give more space to the garden they want to build there, but I don't want to leave. The small piece of land and the hut belongs to my forefathers and I want to keep it because it makes me feel less lonely and reminds me of them. Please, sire, I am not doing anything wrong. Will you support me?'

'If what you say is true, I will,' said the king.

The king sent his men to find out more about the matter and came to know that the poor man was telling the truth—it was the land next to his new palace. Meanwhile, the poor man also found out that the big house being constructed was none other than the king's palace.

'Let it stay,' said the king to his architect. 'I have given the man my word. When people look at the palace, they will see outstanding architecture. When they see the hut, they will also come to know that I am a man of my word.'

In the same kingdom, there lived a zamindar who owned a lot of property. In the old days, people believed that only boys should inherit the property of their parents in the hope that it will bring great name to the family. The zamindar belonged to the old school of thought. When his wife was expecting a baby, she went to live in her parents' house for a few months, as was the custom in those days. As she was leaving, the zamindar told her sternly, 'We must have a son. If you don't give birth to a son, don't come back to stay with me.'

His wife was terrified, but for the sake of the baby, she tried to be positive and happy.

Time passed by quickly and one morning, she delivered a healthy baby girl. She was happy to have a girl, but she was scared of what her husband would do if he found out that she had given birth to a girl!

So she sent word to him, 'I have given birth to a baby boy.'

Perhaps I can convince him to see things from my point of view, once he gets to know our daughter better, she thought.

The ecstatic father sent a message back to her, 'I am pleased. I want to name the boy Veeravara, the brave one.'

Thus, the baby girl was named Veeravara. Her mother helped her keep the secret and so, Veeravara grew up as a boy. She knew that she would have to keep it a secret that she was actually a girl, or face her father's wrath. She wore boyish and loose clothing and got all the necessary education fit for a boy in those days. She was outstanding in archery and horse riding and everyone around her (except her mother) thought that she was actually a boy.*

Two decades passed. When Veeravara was going to another town for work, she had to pass through a forest. There, she saw a man being attacked by a lion. Though the man was fighting back, she knew he needed help. So she leapt to action. She rode her horse towards the man, picked him up quickly and rode away from the lion.

When she stopped the horse, she realized that the man was wounded badly. He told her that he was King Narendra. He had gone to the forest to hunt with his soldiers and had lost his way when he ran into the lion. Quickly, Veeravara brought him back to his palace, handed him over to the royal guards and galloped away.

When the king was in better health, he invited Veeravara to come to his capital as his personal guest. He wanted to thank her for saving his life. Reluctantly, Veeravara agreed since she could not disobey the king's wishes. When she stayed at the palace, the king realized that Veeravara was good at everything she did.

The king had a sister called Chandrika who was stunning and of marriageable age. He thought, *Veeravara is brave and courageous. He may not be a prince, but he is a good man. I would like my sister to marry him.*

The king called Veeravara's parents to discuss the idea. The mother was aghast, but she couldn't reveal the truth to the king. So she said, 'Sire, your sister is a princess and we are ordinary. Besides, we must ask Veeravara's opinion too. He may not want to get married right now.'

Her dominating husband, however, stopped her. He said, 'This is a rare opportunity, sire, where luck has come to us on her own. Our son is handsome and a good warrior. Unfortunately for him, he was born in my family. Otherwise, he is fit to be a royal. I have no objections at all. This marriage has my blessing.'

Thus, the wedding was fixed.

When Veeravara heard the news, she was dumbstruck. But she knew that she didn't have a choice. 'May I spend some time with your sister to understand her thoughts and expectations?' she asked the king.

Princess Chandrika had seen Veeravara a few times in the court. As a young woman, she was enchanted by the warrior. When her brother had suggested her union with Veeravara, she agreed happily. The king replied, 'I know my sister and she agrees with my decision. However, you can spend some time together in the royal gardens, if she is willing.'

Chandrika found Veeravara's request to be an unusual one, but she was happy to spend some time with him and agreed to the request.

Veeravara met Chandrika at the royal gardens and said, 'A princess like you is probably not a good fit for a commoner such as me. I cannot bestow upon you the comforts of a royal family in my house, and I do not want to stay here in the royal court forever. I think the wise decision would be to refuse to marry me.'

Chandrika smiled. 'Wherever you stay with me, it will be like a palace and a loving home in my heart. I don't expect any special treatment in your home.'

Veeravara realized that there was no way she could change Chandrika's mind. She sat down on a bench nearby.

Chandrika said, 'You look concerned. Tell me, what is on your mind?'

'I had a dream yesterday,' said Veeravara.

'Was it so interesting that it is occupying your mind while you are here with me?' she teased him as she sat down too.

'It was a powerful dream. I dreamt that there was a good-looking girl who was always dressed like a boy because of her father's pressure to present a boy to the world. Everyone thought that she was a boy from the day she was born. One day, she was engaged to the king's daughter. Soon, the king's daughter learnt that the boy was, in fact, a girl. "Put her to death," she ordered her guards. Just then, I woke up. The dream was very real, and it really does seem that it is happening to someone, somewhere in the world.

But it left me disturbed. What do you think, princess? Did she do the right thing?'

Chandrika paused for a moment and then said, 'The girl was compelled to be a boy by her parents. It was not of her own free will. So she should not be given the penalty of death. They should release her and allow her to lead a normal life because she might have her own dreams of marriage and children.'

Veeravara stood up and said, 'I am that girl.'

Chandrika was furious. 'How dare you? You could have told me this much earlier and revealed who you are. I will tell my brother. He is sure to kill you for your deceit!'

Frustrated, she began crying.

Veeravara said gently, 'Princess Chandrika, you said that the girl should be released because she had her own pressures and dreams. The moment it became personal, you changed your outlook. I haven't cheated anyone on purpose—neither your brother nor you. Though my mother and I resisted the proposal, nobody listened to us. My father and the rest of the world are in the dark about my gender. That is why I wanted to speak to you alone. If you still think that I deserve the death penalty, I will accept the punishment.'

Chandrika calmed down and felt sorry for Veeravara. She said, 'Perhaps you are right. I can accept this, but if my brother learns of this, he is sure to execute you. Luckily for you, I know how to handle my brother. Come with me tomorrow, but let me lead the discussion.'

The next day, the two women met the king. Narendra was happy to see them together. 'Tell me, what did you two speak about yesterday?' he asked.

Chandrika replied, 'Brother, we spoke about Veeravara's friend. A good-looking girl who was always dressed like a boy because of her father's pressure to present a boy to the world. Everyone thought that she was a boy from the day she was born. One day, she was engaged to the king's daughter. Soon, the king's daughter learnt that the boy was, in fact, a girl. "Put her to death," she ordered her guards. It was all very disturbing. What do you think, brother? Did she do the right thing?'

The king thought for some time and said, 'It is the father, and not the girl, who must be punished. The girl shouldn't even be eligible for punishment.'

Veeravara stepped forward. 'Before we discuss this further, it reminds me of something else I wanted to speak to you about. Sire, I want assurance from you.

I saved your life, and I hope that you will protect my father and ensure that no harm will come to him.'

'Of course, no harm will befall him, Veeravara. He is soon going to be my brother-in-law's father.'

Once he had the king's word, Veeravara revealed the truth, 'Sire, I am that girl.'

The king was livid. 'How dare you? Who do you think you are?'

'Sire, the truth is that I didn't cheat you. I did not ask for your sister's hand in marriage, nor was I keen on the wedding. You were the one who insisted on this match. Please do not hurt my father, though I know that he has done wrong in his ignorance. A daughter can do whatever a son can — I am the best example of this. Your judgement told you that it was not the girl's fault, which means that it is not my fault either. You are a well-respected king because you keep your word, sire. I hope you will understand my perspective. The rest, I leave up to you.'

The king realized that he must keep his word, and also knew deep down in his heart that it was not Veeravara's fault. His anger melted away and he said, 'I see your point. I am sorry for the troubles you have been through, presenting yourself as a man to the world all these years. For a long time, I have had one

123

sister, Chandrika. Today, I adopt you as my sister too and will call you Veerangana. May both of you marry your choice of husbands. I bless you both.'

By the time the story was done, the chapatis were too. Damu helped Ajji pack the chapatis as Ajja called the town officer.

Within minutes, a man was at the gate, waiting to collect the chapatis. He thanked Ajja and Ajji from the gate and Damu ran to handover the food.

'I feel so happy that we could help the labourers!' said Krishna.

Ajja patted her on the head and pulled her rosy cheeks.

*History has revealed to us that Princess Rudrama Devi of the Kakatiya dynasty was raised as a boy and the subjects of the land always thought that the king had a son. This was a rare occurrence, but it did happen. The princess wore men's clothing and trained as a warrior, and later, she fell in love with a prince from the Chalukya dynasty and ruled her kingdom extremely well.

The Language of the Dogs

It was a quiet and hot night. The children were sitting in the veranda under the fan, talking to each other.

A short distance away, Ajja and Kamlu Ajji were sitting on the stairs in comfortable silence, each lost in their own thoughts. They could hear the street dogs barking near the main gate of the house.

'Why do the dogs bark at night?' asked Kamlu Ajji. 'It's the same story in Bangalore too—they start barking in the middle of the night and go on for a really long time.'

'They also have their own problems,' said Ajja. 'Usually, the dogs are fed leftover food from restaurants. But these days, no hotels are open during the lockdown and many are going hungry.'

Sudha Murty

Ajja turned and called out to Ajji who was still inside the house. 'Do you have any food for the dogs?' he yelled.

'A few chapatis and some rice,' she yelled back.

'Bring them here!'

Ajji brought the food and biscuits and went with Ajja and Kamlu Ajji to the main gate. The children watched from a distance. They looked on as two dogs appeared.

Ajji put biscuits, rice and chapati in a bowl and kept water in another bowl just outside the gate. The two dogs looked at her and attacked the food greedily, gobbling it down in minutes. Then they drank the water, wagged their tails to thank her and ran away.

Slowly, the trio walked back and sat on the steps of the veranda. Ajji said, 'I wish they could speak. Then I could make them their favourite food. After all, the earth also belongs to them.'

'Your perspective is so different,' said Ajja. 'Humans can speak and that's why we can do the things we want to and own material things like property and land.'

'Poor animals. We are occupying their land just because they cannot communicate like us. Even if they had ownership of any piece of land before us, they can't tell us.'

'You are right,' said Kamlu Ajji. 'Now that humans are all indoors, lots of animals in India are coming out from the forests to the cities nearest to them because it was all their land a long, long time ago.'

Ajja added, 'This world would have been a different place if we understood the chirping of birds and the language of animals.'

Ajji smiled and said, 'I am thinking of Dheeraj now.'

'Who's Dheeraj?' asked Ajja.

'Do you want to listen to a story?'

Ajja and Kamlu Ajji nodded their heads like children, eager to listen to what Ajji had to say.

Amit and his wife Preeti were high-ranking officials in their kingdom. They were young, powerful and rich and lived in a mansion by a river. They frequently hosted official celebrations on their yacht or their beautiful large gardens, but made sure they invited only those people from the kingdom who were also rich or powerful, and not whom they considered less fortunate.

Ramu was a housekeeper who lived with them and served them for years. One day, he brought home a young boy of six years. The boy looked innocent and intelligent.

Ramu asked Preeti, 'I met this boy in the village fair. He doesn't have anyone to take care of him. I would like to help him. Can he live with me?'

Preeti glanced at the boy and said, 'Sure, as long as he works for us and does not spoil the premises.'

And that is how Dheeraj began living in Preeti and Amit's home.

One day, Amit hosted a dinner for an important minister. The evening began with a tour of the river on the yacht. Then the yacht docked on the riverside, and music began playing as the celebrations commenced in the beautiful gardens. There was a wide spread of delicacies being served. Dheeraj was assisting Ramu with his chores.

The dinner was in full swing when the barking of two dogs disturbed Amit and his guests. The dogs were right outside the main gate of the gardens. Amit gave instructions to Ramu to hush them and chase them away, but the dogs refused to move. The non-stop barking upset Amit and he said, 'I wish someone could understand what they are saying so that we could respond appropriately and ask them to leave.'

Dheeraj was nearby and overheard Amit. Timidly, he approached the master of the house and said, 'Sir, I can understand them.'

Some of the guests laughed while others passed sarcastic comments.

Preeti asked, 'Tell me, boy, what are they saying?'

'Madam, I will tell you if you promise me that you will not get upset when I share their words with you,' said Dheeraj, looking worried.

'They must be talking about food, boy! Anyway, hurry up and tell us,' said Preeti firmly.

'Madam, they are not talking about food.'

'Get to the point, boy! I am losing patience with you,' snapped Amit.

Nervously, Dheeraj continued, 'Sir, there is a male dog and a female dog at the gate. The male dog said, "Look at life's irony."

'"What do you mean?" said the female dog.

'"This couple is used to being served by someone all the time. But a day will come when the master of this house will give an important person water to wash their hands and the lady will voluntarily run and bring a towel for him to wipe his hands."

'"Who are you talking about? Whom will this couple serve?"

'"The male dog grinned and said, "This little boy."

'Both the dogs then had a hearty laugh,' said Dheeraj, and fell silent.

The silence spread through the guests and it ruined their mood.

'Are you mad? You are nothing but a servant boy, an orphan and a poor fellow. You don't have anything to call your own. There is no way we will ever serve you,' retorted Preeti in anger.

Amit was livid. 'This is all nonsense. I don't believe that you can understand the dogs' language. It is just wishful thinking on your part, something you dream of. Be quiet!'

Amit called Ramu immediately and instructed him, 'Take this boy away.'

Dheeraj pleaded, 'Sir, I am not making this up. I have only repeated what I heard.'

Amit refused to look at him.

Quietly, Ramu escorted the boy downstairs, upset and sad. He said, 'My child, don't say such things in front of the masters. They are powerful and can throw you out of the house. Then where will you stay and who will look after you?'

'But, Uncle, I have shared the truth. There was nothing to hide.'

'Do you really understand the language of the dogs?' asked Ramu.

'I can understand their language, but I also know that I can use this skill only three times in my life.'

After the party, Amit and Preeti took Ramu aside. Amit said, 'Dheeraj is no longer allowed to live with us or work for us. Once he falls asleep, take the boy and leave him where you found him.'

Ramu could not disobey Amit, but he was heartbroken. When Dheeraj was sleeping, he put him on a small makeshift boat with some food and a note that read: *Please look after this orphan boy. He has been abandoned through no fault of his own.*

When Dheeraj woke up and realized he had been set adrift on the river, he saw that the boat was going downstream. He was hungry and ate some food, but didn't know what to do after that. By then, the stream had reached the sea and the boat was becoming wobbly.

A big merchant ship was sailing nearby and the captain of the ship spotted the boat through his binoculars. He noticed the boy and sent a rescue team to the boat. Dheeraj was rescued soon and brought back to the ship. The captain met the boy and read the note his team had found. The boy's innocence captured the captain's heart and he decided to let the boy stay and help him. Days passed and the boy began learning skills such as navigation, business knowledge and trade.

One day, when the ship was docked and being readied to set sail again, the captain noticed that Dheeraj looked worried. 'What is the matter?' he asked.

'Sir, I heard a conversation between two dogs,' he said and pointed to two wild dogs sitting a short distance away. 'I urge you to stop all travel today, especially if you are carrying valuable goods.'

'Explain yourself.'

'The two dogs are chatting about a big storm that is going to hit us in twenty-four hours. The birds have warned them that it will destroy everything in its path.'

'Do you understand what they are saying?' asked the captain, surprised at this revelation.

'Yes, but I can do so only three times in my life. I was kicked out the last time I shared my knowledge. I don't know what you will do, but please listen to me and delay the trip by a day.'

The captain laughed. 'I am a seasoned captain. I know when a storm is coming. Now is not the time, and I don't agree with you.'

'Sir, I am not lying. I request you to reconsider. What is the worst that can happen if you delay by a day?'

'I will lose one whole working day and I am under a lot of pressure for a speedy delivery of these expensive goods. I will have to pay my crew for an extra day too and it will affect my profits,' said the captain.

'But isn't life more important?'

'What if there is no storm tomorrow?'

'Then you can punish me. But I guarantee that there will be a storm soon. Besides, have I ever asked you for anything in the time that you have known me?' said Dheeraj.

The captain thought about it and agreed to delay the departure by a day.

The neighbouring ship, however, was loaded with goods and was about to leave. The captain ran to the ship to advise the other captain and convince him to delay his journey by a day too. But the captain there laughed at him. 'You are a well-travelled man. There is no sign of a storm. I am definitely leaving.'

The captain came back, dejected. He waited for a few hours and then suddenly, out of nowhere, he saw huge waves in the distance. They were so huge that they blocked the sun when they rose. Dark clouds

gathered and it started pouring. From his binoculars, the captain saw the neighbouring ship sinking, but there was nothing he could do to stop it.

Later, he thanked the boy profusely and realized that Dheeraj was gifted. Soon, Dheeraj became the apple of his eye.

Years passed and Dheeraj turned into a young man, well versed in trade and the navigation of ships.

One day, the captain, Dheeraj and the crew reached an island known for encouraging business and trade. Dheeraj and the captain went to visit the king, taking some gifts along with them.

The king enjoyed Dheeraj's company since he was smart and an expert in his field. Soon, they were deep in discussion. While speaking, Dheeraj heard two dogs barking nearby.

The king remarked, 'They are quite dear to me, but I am tired of their barking. They refuse to move. I have closed the window, but I can still hear them barking away out there. Usually, they are well behaved.'

The captain looked at Dheeraj.

Dheeraj smiled. He turned to the king and said, 'Sire, I can understand the language of your dogs. Can you open the window so I can hear them clearly?'

'I have never met anyone who can understand what dogs say, but if you are right, I will make you a minister in my court,' said the king.

'Sire, I will do this but not for the greed of being elevated to a minister of the court. I was punished the first time I used it and rewarded the next time. I can use this skill only once more and this will be the last time.'

Dheeraj said, 'There are three dogs down there—a father, a mother and a child. They have been arguing about whom the child belongs to—the father or the mother. The father says the child belongs to him, the mother says the child belongs to her, but the child wishes to let you, the king, decide. He says he will respect your decision. So they are trying to communicate with you.'

The king went to the window and looked at the three dogs below. 'Ah! Their child belongs to the clan,' said the king. 'Yes, a child owes a lot to the parents, but he also has a responsibility to his clan and society.'

With the king's words, the dogs stopped barking, bowed their heads and walked away.

The king was happy and rewarded Dheeraj. He said, 'I want you to become the minister of business. You are intelligent, balanced and mature.'

The captain agreed to free Dheeraj of his duties on the ship. He was proud that the boy was being recognized for his skills.

Months passed and the king remained happy with Dheeraj's service.

One day, the king called him and said, 'Dheeraj, visit all the provinces in our kingdom and see how business is doing. Based on your report, we will fix the rate of taxes throughout the kingdom.'

Dheeraj began his journey. Word spread among the people: 'Dheeraj, the minister of business, is visiting the kingdom everywhere. He will assess the situation on the ground and evaluate the businesses. He'll then provide his inputs to the king about the tax rates.'

Dheeraj reached the province where Amit and Preeti lived, and a vague memory came to his mind when he saw their mansion, the river and the yacht. Dheeraj's mind raced at this discovery. He learnt that Amit had gone up the ladder even further and had become a top official. Dheeraj decided to focus on his work and not mention his time there.

The next day, Amit hosted a big lunch with a lot of guests, in Dheeraj's honour.

After lunch, Dheeraj went to wash his hands in the sink. Suddenly, Amit came out with a jug of water since there were no taps in those days. Soon, his wife Preeti also came running out with a towel. It was vital to please the king's official and be as hospitable as they could, so that they could gain future benefits.

Dheeraj washed and wiped his hands and looked out from the balcony. He saw the servant's quarters and saw Ramu working below.

He laughed a little, surprising everyone. Then he asked, 'Will you call that man here?'

'Sir, he is only a servant. He can't give you any information about our business,' said Preeti.

'But I must meet him,' Dheeraj responded.

The guests were stunned. They had assumed that Dheeraj would want to spend time getting to know the business people in the province, but he wanted to speak to a mere servant!

Ramu was called. He had grown old and frail. When he entered the room, Dheeraj embraced him, 'Uncle, how are you? I never thought I would see you again. You are partially responsible for who I am today.'

No one understood what he was talking about. Ramu stared at Dheeraj and after a few seconds, he realized who he was. Tears filled his eyes.

With an arm around Ramu's shoulder, Dheeraj turned to the guests and said, 'Twenty-five years ago, I was a poor orphan. Ramu uncle took me in and I worked in this house for a while. I heard two dogs talking during one such celebration. They said that a day would come when Amit-ji would bring water and Preeti-ji would bring a towel for me to wash my hands. Today, this has come true. In their anger, they had told Ramu uncle to abandon me. Poor uncle was in no position to refuse their request, so he put me on a boat when I was asleep and sent me across the river with a kind note. My foster father, the captain of a ship, adopted me and looked after me well. It is his and Uncle's compassion and kindness that made me who I am today.'

Nobody said a word.

Dheeraj took Ramu by the hand and walked out of the room.

By the time Ajji finished the story, she saw all the children sitting behind her, listening intently. They had been there the whole time!

Raghu grinned. 'Ajja and Kamlu Ajji, do you think you can hear the stories without us? The moment we heard the word "story", we came running from the veranda to listen to Ajji.'

April Showers Bring May Flowers

The day was hot and humid. Damu looked at the sky and said, 'It will rain today!'

'How do you know that?' asked Aditi.

'April always brings showers,' he replied.

For the children, Damu was an important link to the outside world. He was the one who would go to the market, buy groceries and other essentials, return and keep things out in the sun to sanitize them. Then he would go for a bath and join the family after he was clean and fresh again.

'What's happening outside in the town?' asked Krishna.

'Everything is closed. There are few people on the road and only a few shops are open for groceries, medicines, vegetables and of course, petrol bunks too. People get out of the house only to buy things they need urgently.'

'Do you get mangoes in the market?' queried Raghu.

'Not yet. See the mango trees there?' said Damu, pointing to the trees inside the compound. 'The mangoes are still raw.'

'Then when will ripe mangoes be available in the market?' persisted Raghu. He loved mangoes.

'Usually, you get the best mangoes in the month of May. But when rain falls, things are not the same. For instance, when rain falls in April, the mangoes fall and the yield is less. That is why mango growers don't like April showers, but people who grow jackfruit prefer it because the quality of the fruit gets better with the rain.'

Ajji joined the conversation. 'April showers bring May flowers,' she remarked.

'Yes, Bangalore also has red flowers that bloom in May,' piped in Anoushka.

'There are many flowers that bloom after April showers, especially those that are used to manufacture herbal medicines since the herbs grow better with the natural rain in April.'

'How do you know that, Ajji?' asked Meenu.

'One of my friends is a doctor of Ayurveda. He told me. After April showers, he would go to the forest in search of medicinal flowers, leaves and fruits.'

'What else did he say?'

'Well, he also told me a story.'

'I also want to know about these herbs. Wait a minute, I have just put the pressure cooker on the gas. Give me a few minutes and I will also join in,' yelled Kamlu Ajji from the kitchen.

Soon, everyone had settled in to listen to the story that Ajji had heard from the Ayurvedic doctor.

Mahesh was a popular doctor in his village, and had immense knowledge about herbs and medicines.

Within a few years, he became famous in the village and the surrounding areas. Unfortunately, he also became arrogant and frequently said, 'I can cure any disease in the world. If I can't cure it, then the disease is incurable.'

One day, a man named Prashant came to him with an unusual fever. No matter what medicines Mahesh gave him, they didn't help and Prashant remained ill.

After two months, Mahesh gave up and said, 'Look, my man, this disease cannot be cured. Pray to God to save you.'

Prashant went home, desperate and dejected. Mahesh called his wife and said, 'Take care of your husband. I have tried my best and failed. I don't think he will survive more than a few weeks.'

Months passed. One day, Mahesh went to the market to shop for groceries and ran into Prashant—he looked hale and hearty and was busy managing a shop in the market. Mahesh was surprised. How on earth was this patient still alive? He approached Prashant and said, 'I am glad to see you. How are you?'

'As you can see, I have completely recovered and I am so thankful!'

'Which doctor treated you after me?' asked Mahesh.

'Sometimes, a doctor appears in the form of God. Even if the doctor only gives water, it can be as good as the best medicine for the patient,' said Prashant.

Mahesh was annoyed. 'Well, then, tell me the name of the God that cured you.'

'A lady called Hema lives across the river. She treats patients with her own medicines and I went to her as a last resort. She gave me five tablets and I recovered fully by the time I had finished the last dose.'

Mahesh forgot all about his grocery shopping and went home thinking about Hema.

That night, he couldn't sleep a wink. *She couldn't be better than him, could she?*

The next morning, he crossed the river and asked a few people for directions to Hema's house. Many people seemed to have heard of her and pointed him in the right direction. When he reached, he saw that she had a tiny two-room house. Outside, there was a small makeshift hut that had been turned into a clinic. That's where Hema treated her patients.

Mahesh refused to wait in line. He went up to Hema and introduced himself, 'I am Mahesh, a famous doctor from across the river. I met your patient Prashant yesterday. I had tried to cure him a few months ago, but all my medicines failed. He must have come to you after that. Now he looks strong and healthy. What did you give him?'

'Please sit, doctor,' said Hema and invited him inside.

'No, I don't have much time. Please tell me quickly and briefly—in one sentence. I will be able to understand.

145

I have a feeling that it may be just luck. There are many times when diseases can cure themselves and the doctor gets the credit for the cure anyway,' said Mahesh.

Hema laughed. 'Maybe,' she said.

'Tell me what you gave him,' insisted Mahesh.

'I'll keep it brief for you then—April showers bring May flowers,' she replied as she called in her next patient, dismissing Mahesh.

Mahesh left. *May flowers*, he thought. *It must be easy to understand.*

He went to the market and bought flowers that bloom in May. But there seemed to be no medicinal effect in helping fever or any other typical symptoms.

He became obsessed with Hema's words. Finally, he thought about taking someone's help and approached a literature expert.

'April showers bring May flowers,' he said to the expert.

'What a lovely phrase,' said the expert. 'I don't get anything else out of it, my friend.'

Then Mahesh went to a florist, who said, 'May flowers are very beautiful indeed. All I can tell you is that I sell a lot of these flowers.'

That didn't help Mahesh either.

Next, he went to an artist friend. The artist said, 'It is soothing and inspirational to paint both April showers and May flowers.'

That turned out to be a dead end too.

Frustrated, Mahesh decided to return home. As he made his way back home, he passed two farmers talking about their crops. One of them remarked, 'The best crop is right after the monsoon. The rain brings the best quality of food. Even if there is continuous irrigation or a source of water nearby, there is nothing like the monsoon showers. The quality of the crop is outstanding with the natural rain. It is a gift from the gods above and I am always grateful!'

Suddenly, Mahesh realized what Hema meant. The medicinal plants that flower after the April showers have a high medicinal value, and only those flowers are recommended for use while preparing medicines.

He went across the river right away, to Hema's house and explained what he had discovered. He asked her, 'Have I understood your words correctly?'

She smiled. 'Yes, use only those flowers that bloom after the rain in April. After May, the medicinal value reduces in the flowers but gets transferred and goes deep into the roots. So don't use flowers after that. Instead, you can use a different part of the plant or tree.

This way you are sure to have herbs and medicines throughout the year.'

'Why didn't you tell me all this the first time I came?'

'You said you had time for only one sentence.' Hema chuckled.

Mahesh realized the error of his ways. 'I may be a good doctor, but there are also others as good as me, or even better than me. Knowledge is never limited—it can come from anywhere and I must keep an open mind.'

He thanked Hema and said, 'Will you take me as your student and teach me what you know? I will share my limited knowledge with you too.'

She smiled and nodded. 'Let's work together. I'd really like that.'

Ajji ended the story and said, '*Aushadhi Jahnavi Toyam Vaidyo Narayano Harihi*. This Sanskrit shloka says that when we have medicine, we must consider it sacred—like water from the river Ganga. The lord comes to us in the form of a doctor who gives us medicines, and we must have it with the same faith.'

Damu and the children nodded solemnly, agreeing with her.

That evening, there was a heavy downpour of rain. Later, the children ran outside to see what had happened to the mangoes in the trees inside the compound.

Damu was right—the small mangoes along with mango flowers lay on the ground like a yellow carpet. And the tree seemed to be smiling at them—green and fresh.

The Case of the Mystery Pot

One morning, Ajji was making pulao, which was almost everyone's favourite.

After some time, Ajji came out of the kitchen and said, 'I am going with Kamlu to check on the cows. We will also feed them while we are there. Kids, I have finished cooking, but don't open the pressure cooker just yet. Let it settle and cool on its own. We will have lunch as soon as I am back.'

The children nodded as they were busy completing their homework.

Ajji left and a few minutes passed.

'Why is vegetable rice called pulao?' asked Raghu suddenly, a tad thoughtful.

'Pulao originated from Uzbekistan,' answered Ajja. 'Originally, leftover vegetables along with rice and some masala were cooked over slow fire in an earthen pot. This was usually done for soldiers as the food was nutritious and minimal oil was needed. They also used a sort of plate made of wheat flour to cover the pot. Later the recipe was modified and today, pulao is cooked all over India with different ingredients. Tell me, have any of you read about any other food that has become internationally famous?'

'Minestrone soup,' said Raghu. 'One day, I went out with Dad and Mom to an Italian restaurant. They ordered minestrone soup, which I found difficult to pronounce at first. After I came home and googled it, I found out that leftover rice was cooked with some herbal vegetables and made into a soup. Farmers could drink this in the mornings and go to work since it was light and nutritious. From there to now, it is known the world over with each country customizing it their way and making it their own.'

'Very good, Raghu.' Ajja beamed.

That's when Ajja noticed that Aditi and Meenu were missing. Ajja stood up slowly and carefully so as not to disturb the other three children. He was going to go look for the two girls.

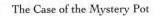

Meanwhile, Aditi and Meenu were feeling ravenous and couldn't resist following the aroma of the pulao, which led them to the kitchen.

Aditi whispered, 'Ajji has instructed us not to open the lid!'

'Don't be scared, Aditi. We will only open it a little.'

When Meenu opened the lid, there was a loud boom. They tried to run out of the kitchen in such a hurry that they both slipped. Ajja heard the noise and rushed in to find Meenu and Aditi on the floor and the cooker whistling away. He understood what had happened. He found the nozzle of the pressure cooker and put it back on the cooker.

Then he reached out both hands and pulled up Meenu and Aditi.

'We just wanted to open it a little, Ajja,' whimpered Aditi. 'We are fine. Nothing has happened to us.'

Ajja smiled. 'Curiosity kills the cat. Let me tell you something.'

A long, long time ago, there lived a wise king. One day, he went hunting all alone. And when he was on his way back, it began raining. So the king found a dry spot in the veranda of a nearby hut, which belonged to a poor old woodcutter and his wife.

As the king waited outside, he heard the couple speaking to each other. The wife said, 'The hut is so old that it is falling apart and we have no food to eat. We are shivering too. There is no point trying to find work. Who will give us a job? Think of our king—he gets clean and warm clothes and good food every day. I wish we had that.'

'Don't worry. At least we are together,' said the woodcutter, trying to console his wife. 'We will do the best we can.'

The king couldn't resist himself any more and knocked on the door. When the couple opened the door, he said, 'I heard your conversation. I will ensure that you get warm clothes and good food. But will you accompany me back to the palace?'

The couple was pleasantly surprised. 'Yes, of course,' said the wife.

'There is one condition,' said the king. 'You must obey me. The day you don't do so, you will be back here.'

'Your Majesty, if we get good food, warm clothing and a place to stay, we will never question you,' said the wife vehemently.

The woodcutter also nodded in agreement.

'In that case, lock your home and follow me. The rain has stopped and we will leave now,' instructed the king.

The wife locked the house and tucked the key away safely. The couple then followed the king. After walking for what seemed like a long time, they reached the palace.

The king ordered one of his trusted servants to take care of them, 'This man and his wife are my personal guests. Look after them very well.'

Saying this, the king left, and the couple was left alone with the servant. The servant took them to a nice room that had warm food on the table and a water heater. There were even silk robes in the bathroom! The couple took a warm bath and pulled on the robes. They were about to sit down to dinner when the king walked in, 'How do you like your room? Is it warm enough?' he asked.

'Sir, we could not have dreamt of such a hospitable stay,' said the old woodcutter. 'It is beyond our imagination.'

'Of course. You are my subjects. You can eat whatever you want and whatever you wish. But there is a small pot in your room with a lid on it. You must never open it. The day you open it, you will have to go back to your hut,' said the king firmly.

'Why will we need to open it when you have given us so much comfort?' said the wife with a grateful smile.

The king chatted with them for a few more minutes and left.

At first, the couple was ecstatic at the opportunity to experience the palace and all that it had to offer — the royal gardens, the massive kitchen, sweet fruits and exquisite flowers.

After a few weeks, the wife glanced at the pot and said out loud, 'I wonder what is inside.'

'My dear wife, how does it matter as long as we have enough?'

After a few days, with nothing else to do, the wife said again, 'I am really curious to know what is inside the pot.'

Her husband refused to open it, but she didn't give up. She kept pestering her husband, who said harshly, 'I have given my word to the king.'

The wife became unhappier as the days went by. She ate less. She talked less. She thought about the pot all the time.

Then she began fighting with her husband to open the lid of the pot.

Meanwhile, the king continued to visit them but noticed that they were no longer happy.

One day, while talking to the servant, the woodcutter's wife heard that the king had gone hunting to the forest and was expected to come back only after a week. She went to her husband and said, 'Dear, come, let's open the pot just a little bit. We will peep inside and close it quickly. No one will ever know.'

'But we will know. What is the point of all this, dear? Why should we disobey the king? He has been kind to us and we have no reason to betray his trust.'

The wife was adamant, 'No, I must know.'

Finally, the woodcutter gave in and lifted the lid of the pot. Smoke came out all of a sudden and the woodcutter dropped the lid with a loud clatter.

Within seconds, the servant came inside and knew what had happened. Minutes later, the king

had also joined them, much to the couple's dismay. It seemed that news about him having gone hunting had been false. The king said, 'You did not obey me. An idle person has nothing to do, which raises their curiosity about matters that are of no concern to them.' He looked at the wife, 'You have the key to your hut. I will give you some food and fruits to last you for some time. Go back to your home and try to find work—it will keep you both healthy and happy.'

This is how curiosity destroyed their comfortable and luxurious life.

Meenu asked, 'So we shouldn't be curious at all and always listen to others?'

'No, I didn't say that. Curiosity in the right direction leads to innovation and entrepreneurship, but if it is in the wrong direction, it has the potential to hurt other people and you. It also means that you must not intrude on someone's privacy.'

Meenu and Aditi looked at each other and felt ashamed.

The Gold, the Bride and
the Dancing Tiger

One day, Ajja thought that the family should have a picnic in the garden for a change.

The children decided to assist that day, with Damu and Ajja's cooking expertise, and they insisted that Ajji and Kamlu Ajji relax and do as they pleased.

Damu was an expert cook while Ajja was just an ordinary one. The children, who had no knowledge of cooking, decided to make something simple and fun.

Ajja suggested, 'I have an electric tandoor that I brought from Punjab during my visit there. We can make roti, dal, raita and rice.'

'That sounds yummy, Ajja,' said Aditi.

'While we set it up, why don't you go and clean the area where we will have the picnic?'

'Yes, of course, Ajja!'

Together, the children helped clean the area under the mango tree. Raghu laid out mats, Krishna brought out plates and water, Meenu brought out spoons and ladles and Aditi brought towels and soaps. Anoushka arranged fruits and sweets.

In the kitchen, Ajja had finished kneading the dough while Damu was in the middle of cooking both dal and a dry vegetable side by side.

The children saw the tandoor and found the iron rod with a hook quite amusing. They enjoyed the process of cooking rotis in the tandoor. 'Taking out the rotis from the tandoor is not easy, kids. It takes an expert to know and do this,' said Ajja, proudly.

It took some time for the fresh rotis to be made but soon, the group sat down to eat lunch.

'Such good rotis,' said Krishna. 'I love rotis!'

'I like dessert,' said Meenu.

'I like dal,' said Raghu.

Everyone managed to eat something that they really, really liked.

'Some people are happy with food, some with clothes and some with animals,' remarked Damu.

'Do animals dance?' asked Krishna.

'Sometimes. I have seen dogs dancing,' he replied.

Ajja said, 'I have seen a horse dancing.'

'I have seen a bear dance,' said Raghu.

'Well, I know of a tiger that dances,' said Damu.

'Really?' asked Anoushka. 'Where? Is he in this village?'

'I am scared,' said Meenu and looked horrified.

'Nonsense, Damu!' said Ajja. 'There is no such thing.'

'There is,' said Damu. 'I had heard a story about such a tiger when I was very young.'

There once lived a pious old man in a village who often helped others. He had three sons.

One day, he fell ill and knew that he was on his deathbed. He called his sons, Ram, Shyam and Shashi, and said to them, 'I don't have too much to leave for you except for three things—a round stone grinder, a big horn of an animal and a drum.'

He gave the grinder to his oldest son Ram, the empty, hollow horn to his second son Shyam and the drum to his third son Shashi.

Within a few days, the old man passed away.

The three brothers took their gifts and departed from the village. Soon, they came to a crossroads. Each one decided to take a different road. 'Let us meet back here after a year to see what we did with our gifts and how it was useful to us,' said Ram.

Shyam and Shashi agreed and went their own ways.

Ram walked miles until it was evening. He was exhausted. From a distance, he saw a lamp but did not have the energy to walk all the way there.

So he stopped near a banyan tree and decided that it was safe enough for him to sleep on top of the branches, instead of on the ground. He held the grinder with both arms and slept between the branches.

Hours later, he woke up, startled. He heard voices underneath the branches and realized that two thieves were in a deep discussion about the wealth they had just looted and how they planned to divide it. Ram became afraid and worried about the thieves finding him. In his nervousness, he touched the wooden handle of the grinder and made a full circle with it.

As there was nothing inside to grind, there was a loud harsh noise.

KRRRRRRRRRR!

The thieves looked up, afraid, but in the dark night, they could not see anything. They looked on either side of the tree, but there was nothing there either.

'Did you hear that?' asked one of the thieves.

'Was that a monster? Perhaps one that lives in the tree? I have heard from many people that banyan trees can have monsters living in them.'

'That is not true.'

Ram realized they were very afraid of the sound the grinder made, so he turned the wooden handle two more times.

KRRRRRRRRRR! KRRRRRRRRRR!

The thieves stood up.

Ram repeated it again, and again and again. The sound was much louder and harsher than before. The thieves became terrified and ran away leaving their loot under the tree.

Ram waited for a few hours until it was early morning and came down from the tree. He found that the thieves had left two heavy bags of gold and jewellery. Ram took the bags and walked away.

He thanked his father in his mind for giving him the stone grinder, with the help of which he had now become a very rich man.

Now, the second brother Shyam had followed his path and reached the outskirts of a village. He wanted to reach the village quickly, but it began raining heavily. *I will go there tomorrow morning*, he thought.

So he stopped near a banyan tree and decided that it was safe enough for him to sleep among its branches, instead of on the ground. He hid the horn in the hole of the tree trunk and slept between the branches.

In the middle of the night, he heard two people speaking quietly to each other under the banyan tree. One said, 'I have done an excellent job today. The village headman's daughter had her birthday celebrations and I was given the task of making many delicacies for the party. I have followed your instructions and added the medicine to her food. It will make her stay deep in sleep all night.'

'Wonderful,' said the second man. 'She won't get up till the evening tomorrow and until then, people will think that she is dead. That will be when we go and offer to give her this medicine to wake her up. The headman will be happy after she is awake and he may ask what we want. I will tell him that I want to marry his daughter. Once we are married, I will give you plenty of money.'

Shyam understood that the two men below the tree were a cook and a crook plotting against an innocent girl. He felt pity for the girl whom he had not even seen.

The crook said, 'I have had a hard day at work, so let us rest here till the morning. But we need to hide the medicine before we sleep.'

'Look,' said the cook. 'There is a hole in the trunk of the tree. Keep the medicine there. No one will think of checking there and we can sleep without a worry in the world.'

The crook reached out his hand and kept the medicine in the horn hidden in the hole of the tree trunk, and the two men finally settled under the tree. There was a cool breeze in the air and the men began snoring within minutes.

Shyam knew what he had to do. Early the next morning, he got down from the tree, picked up the horn and the medicine that was lying inside it. He quickly walked to the village ahead but kept mum. He wanted to confirm what the men had said.

Soon enough, there was a commotion in the village market.

'The birthday girl refuses to wake up!' someone said.

'She looks dead but she isn't!' said another.

The village doctor was called but was unsuccessful in rousing her. As she was the only child of the village headman, the entire family was in tears. The headman begged the crowd surrounding his house, 'Is there anyone who can wake my daughter up? I will give them whatever they want. We cannot live without her!'

Shyam observed this for some time and then walked up to the headman and said, 'I will try to cure her.'

He took the medicine and put it in the girl's mouth until she had swallowed it. Within a few minutes, she woke up.

There was joy all around. People hugged him and shook his hands, thanking him profusely. The headman offered Shyam a lot of money for saving his daughter's life, but he refused.

He took the headman aside and told him what he had heard the previous night and the sequence of events. The headman welcomed his honesty and said, 'You are a young and a helpful man. Perhaps you are the best man worthy of my daughter. I would like the two of you to be wed. If you agree, we can perform the engagement ceremony today.'

This is how Shyam agreed to marry the village headman's daughter, who also liked the handsome young man.

The cook and the crook woke up late afternoon and searched high and low for the medicine. It was not there in the hole of the tree trunk. They were certain that nobody could have stolen it. So they assumed that a bird may have flown off with it, and nobody in the village would know about their plan.

Satisfied that they would be safe if they returned to the village, they walked back. From a distance, they saw that there were festivities in the village. The cook stopped a passer-by and asked, 'What is going on there?'

'Aren't you the cook of the house?' said the man. 'Don't you know? The daughter of the headman is getting engaged this evening. A young man saved her life using a special medicine.'

'How is that possible?' wondered both the men.

When they approached the headman's house, they were surrounded by the police and arrested.

'What have I done?' asked the cook.

'I don't even know this village,' said the crook.

The headman stepped forward, exposed their plot and the police escorted them to jail. The puzzled look on their faces spoke volumes — they still didn't understand how the medicine reached the headman's house.

Meanwhile, Shashi took the road that led to the forest. It was already dark. So he stopped under a banyan tree and decided that it was safe enough for him to sleep among the branches, instead of on the ground. He couldn't fall asleep, so he began to play the drum.

To his surprise, a tiger came and stood under the banyan tree. He seemed to have a thorn in his paw, which was very painful. After some time, the tiger wanted to climb the tree and attack Shashi, but he couldn't. He fell down again and again. During his efforts to climb and find a grip, the thorn fell out of the paw and the tiger's pain was immediately relieved.

For a few minutes, the tiger listened to the continuous drumming and feeling relaxed, he began dancing. Shashi found it amusing. The more he drummed, the more the tiger danced. Shashi was afraid to stop drumming in case the tiger changed its mind and attacked him. So he drummed the whole night and the tiger danced until it was exhausted and slept in the wee hours of the morning.

Slowly, Shashi came down from the tree and was just about to make his exit when the tiger stirred and opened his eyes. Shashi thought, *Oh no! He will kill me now!*

The tiger, however, did not harm him.

When he walked away, the tiger followed him.

Shashi played the drum while walking and noticed that whenever he drummed, the tiger danced. Whenever he stopped, the tiger followed him and did not attack. That's when Shashi realized that the tiger liked him and was happy to be with him.

Soon, Shashi had made his way out of the forest. He entered a village, but the people saw the tiger around him and ran away. Shashi pleaded, 'Please don't be afraid. Come close. I will beat my drum and the tiger will dance for you.'

At first, people were sceptical, but then they saw him beat the drum and the tiger dance. They gave him some money for entertaining them.

In the evening, Shashi and the tiger went back to the forest. Shashi ate food and again slept on a branch of the banyan tree.

This became his routine. The tiger joined him when he got down from the tree in the morning, and together, they went to different villages and towns and the tiger would dance to the beat of his drum. They would come back to the forest in the evening.

In time, other animals in the forest also became Shashi's friends.

Soon, a king heard news of the tiger whisperer and sent word to Shashi to come and perform for him at the capital. Politely, Shashi sent word back through the king's messengers, 'The tiger has to return to the forest in the evening, and we cannot make the journey to the capital as it is a long distance away. I will be grateful if the king comes here to see our unique show.'

The king understood the relationship of the tiger with the forest. So he came and enjoyed the dance of the tiger.

He told Shashi, 'I have a forest close to the capital city. I will give you ten thousand gold coins if the tiger and you live there. Then you can perform the show in my court regularly.'

Shashi replied, 'Sir, the tiger is a part of my family. His comfort is important. He is not for sale, just like this drum, which is a gift from my father. Whenever you want to see him, please come here. I promise that we will always entertain you.'

The king was pleased that Shashi had considered the animal as a part of his family and was not money-minded. 'I salute you, young man,' he said, 'for caring so deeply for animals. There are few men in the world like you. Here, take this, I would still like to give you some money. I will come when I can.'

The king gave Shashi some gold coins and returned to his palace.

A year passed and the three brothers met again at the crossroads of their village. They shared their stories and thanked their father in heaven for their three special gifts.

'What a wonderful story, Damu!' said Ajja, sounding pleased.

'Yes, Damu, I really enjoyed your story,' said Meenu.

'Thank you, Meenu. I have heard many stories from Ajji while working with her. Sometimes, when I have nothing to do at night, I lie down on the veranda, look at the stars and the sky and create stories. I also have two brothers and that's how I thought of this story.'

A Ship on the Land

One day, Raghu got a call from his friend George in Bangalore.

There were two festivals for which George always invited his friends home—Christmas and Easter. Usually, George's parents hosted a big Easter party every year for all their relatives and friends but not this year. Raghu had been to George's Easter party the year before—there was a wonderful spread of food with lots of cakes, gifts and music. George told him, 'It was so boring this year, Raghu. It was just my parents, my grandmother who has moved in with us for the duration of the lockdown and me. When there are no people, there is no fun in celebrations and festivals. At least you have your cousins with you, I am all alone here.'

George's mother worked in a travel agency and their offices were closed. 'My mother is worried and frustrated,' said George. 'When she works, she is active and full of life. Now, she is restless at home and I am missing all of you.'

'Can you come here for a few days, George?' asked Raghu. 'It will be so much fun and I will finally have my own friend. My grandparents will be pleased to have another child in the house.'

'My grandmother says we must not go anywhere right now,' said George. 'On top of that, my father has placed restrictions on my screen time too. I am waiting for you to come back so that I can see you.'

'Me too. When I come back, I will tell you many stories that I have heard here. Let's call each other frequently,' said Raghu and said goodbye.

A few hours later, Krishna got a call from her friend, Salma. Salma said, 'I am getting really bored here. All the adults above the age of sixty are at my house because my parents are both doctors. Most of our extended family decided to come here. I am the only child, so they focus all their energies on me—why am I not eating, have I done my homework, what I should wear, why I should listen to them—it never ends. It's too much! I am stuck with all these Ajjis at home.

Still, I am happy that my parents are helping people during this time. But I don't know how Eid will be celebrated this year with all this going on. When are you coming back, Krishna? I need a change in my life. I wish I could come there to see you.'

Krishna laughed. 'Here, the number of children are more than the number of adults. Don't worry, Salma. Hang in there. After I come back, I will share many stories to your liking. Once the lockdown ends, I am sure that many of your guests will go back.'

After she had finished the call, Ajji said, 'I am glad that you children have friends you can share things with. With good friends around, one can achieve a lot. But it is difficult to get good friends. Once you get them, don't take the relationship for granted. Look at Kamlu Ajji and me. We are friends because we like each other, and not just because we are relatives and have to. We understand each other and love to chat and work with each other while making each other happy—exactly like Vishnu and his friends.'

'Who is Vishnu, Ajji? Where does he live?' said Krishna.

'Let me tell you about him.'

A long time ago, there lived a king who ruled a great and big kingdom. Since he was a powerful king, he always got what he wanted. After some time, he got bored and thought, *I want to own something unusual.*

One day, while looking out to sea, he saw ships sailing. He wondered, *Why not own a ship that sails on land? No one has ever thought of this!*

Excited about his idea, he made an announcement all over the kingdom, 'Whoever can make me a ship that sails on land will be awarded a royal position in the court.'

People laughed. 'How can that ever happen?' they said. 'A ship, by default, sails only on water.'

There was a carpenter in the kingdom who lived near the woods. He had three intelligent sons. He asked them, 'Why don't you try and work on something that looks like a ship but works on land?'

Early the next morning, the first son Kiran carried some food in a box and set out towards the forest. He came across a fine teakwood tree. He chopped it down and began working on creating a ship.

Once it was time for breakfast, he opened his box. A bumblebee approached him and said, 'I used to live on this teakwood tree. You have cut the tree down and I don't have a home any more. I am starving. Will you share your meal with me?'

Kiran refused, 'I am sorry, but I don't have much to share with you right now. I have much work to do and I need the energy.'

'What are you building?' asked the bumblebee.

'I am making wooden ladles for the king,' said Kiran, since he didn't want to tell her the truth.

'Oh, wooden ladles for the king,' repeated the bumblebee and flew away.

After breakfast, Kiran kept cutting the wood and everything came out in the shape of wooden ladles. He tried until evening but couldn't make anything other than ladles.

Disappointed, he came back home.

The carpenter asked anxiously, 'Did you manage to make anything?'

'No, Father, I couldn't find a suitable tree. The trees were too small and they were fit only for wooden ladles.'

Early the next morning, the second son Sandeep carried some food in a box and set out towards the forest. He came across a fine teakwood tree. He chopped it down and began working on creating a ship.

Once it was time for breakfast, he opened his box. A bumblebee approached him and said, 'I used to live on this teakwood tree. You have cut the tree down and

I don't have a home any more. I am starving. Will you share your meal with me?'

Sandeep refused, 'I am sorry, but I don't have much to share with you right now. I have much work to do and I need the energy.'

'What are you building?' asked the bumblebee.

'I am making wooden plates for the king,' said Sandeep, since he didn't want to tell her the truth.

'Oh, wooden plates for the king,' repeated the bumblebee and flew away.

After breakfast, Sandeep kept cutting the wood and everything came out in the shape of wooden plates. He tried until evening but couldn't make anything other than plates.

Disappointed, he came back home.

The carpenter asked anxiously, 'Did you manage to make anything?'

'No, Father, I couldn't find a suitable tree. The trees were too small and they were fit only for wooden plates.'

Early the next morning, the third son Vishnu carried some food in a box and set out towards the forest. He came across a fine teakwood tree.

Vishnu stood and prayed to the tree. He said, 'I must cut you down for a special project for the king. I am sorry that this will interfere with the life that you have and the living things that surround you. Please forgive me. I will plant twenty other trees to compensate for your loss.'

Saying this, Vishnu chopped the tree down and began working on creating a ship.

Once it was time for breakfast, he opened his box. A bumblebee approached him and said, 'I used to live on this teakwood tree. You have cut the tree down and I don't have a home any more. I am starving. Will you share your meal with me?'

'Of course,' said Vishnu. 'In fact, I must feed you since you have lost your home because of me. Come, let us share.'

Though the bumblebee was small, she ate a lot. After she was full, she said, 'Come, I will also help you. But what are you building?'

'I want to make a ship for the king that can sail on land.'

'Oh, a ship for the king that can sail on land,' repeated the bumblebee and stayed with him.

After breakfast, Vishnu continued to cut the wood. The bumblebee helped him and everything came out in unusual shapes.

At lunch, the bumblebee and Vishnu shared the food. They immediately got back to work and soon, it was evening and the ship was ready. The decorations and interior furniture were also all done. He thanked the bumblebee for her help and began sailing on the road.

On the way, he saw a man drinking water directly from a river. 'What is the matter? Why are you drinking so much water?'

'I am extremely thirsty. No matter how much I drink, it is not enough. It is torturous.'

'Come and join me here on the ship. I am going to hand this over to the king and I will request him to quench your thirst,' said Vishnu, and the man agreed.

They sailed further and saw a man sitting and eating a big pile of apples. 'What are you doing?' Vishnu asked.

'I am famished. No amount of food can satisfy me. It is excruciating.'

'Come and join us here on the ship. I am going to hand this over to the king and I will request him to give you food until you have eaten your fill,' said Vishnu, and the man agreed.

The men sailed further and saw a strong man carrying a huge load of wood on his back. 'What are you doing?' Vishnu asked.

'I have a stepmother who doesn't treat me well unless I bring this much wood home every day. It is exhausting. I just want to earn some money to take care of myself.'

'Come and join us here on the ship. I am going to hand this over to the king and I will request him to help you,' said Vishnu, and the man agreed.

The men sailed further and saw a man sitting and feeding numerous dogs and cats. 'What are you doing?' Vishnu asked.

'I don't have any skills. Whatever I manage to earn, I use it to buy food and feed it to these strays.'

'Come and join us here on the ship. I am going to hand this over to the king and I will request him to help you take care of the strays,' said Vishnu, and the man agreed.

When the five men reached the capital, the king came to see the ship. He was joyous and extremely pleased. Not only was it a sailing ship but the décor was also much better than his palace. He took a tour of the ship, saw how it worked and finally met Vishnu, the carpenter's son. Vishnu wore regular clothing and so did his friends. The king thought, *How can I give a royal position to this ordinary man? I will test him first.*

So he said, 'Vishnu, I want to award you the royal position, but I have some conditions.'

Vishnu nodded.

The king pointed to a big pond of water and said, 'This must be empty by tomorrow morning.'

He pointed to a big pile of bread and said, 'This must be eaten by tomorrow morning.'

He pointed to a group of trees and said, 'All these must be cut into pieces by tomorrow morning.'

He pointed to a big playground and said, 'This must be full of cats and dogs by tomorrow morning.'

Though it wasn't part of the contract or the announcement that was made, Vishnu smiled and said, 'I will try to complete the tasks, sire.'

The king left Vishnu and his friends and went back to his duties for the day.

Vishnu's friends turned to him and said, 'We can do all these things for you. Wait and watch.'

The thirsty man drank all the water from the pond and quenched his thirst.

The hungry man ate all the bread and satisfied his hunger.

The strong man cut the wood in no time and realized that he could make enough money by himself and didn't need to go back to his stepmother.

The kind man whistled and called all his dog and cat friends, filling the playground within minutes.

The next day, when the king came, all the tasks were completed and done well. Vishnu and his friends stood nearby.

The king realized that it is not the appearance or the clothing that matters but the skill and talent of a person. 'I will be honoured to have all of you in my court. The five of you will be given royal positions, you will be my trusted advisers and rewarded handsomely for your work in the court and the kingdom.'

This is how Vishnu made his father proud and made new friends who would stay with him for a lifetime.

Two Blind Beggars

Now almost forty days had passed. Still, the lockdown continued. There were no flights, trains or buses running to take people back home. Many schools had informed parents that online classes would start in June if the situation didn't improve. The children were not looking forward to online classes because they wanted to see their friends and play with them.

Ajja remarked, 'The online classes will lead to excessive screen time—it might cause addiction or at the very least, eye strain. But right now, I can't think of a solution to this problem.'

Ajja closely followed the developments around Covid-19 in India.

One evening, while Ajja was watching the news, the children decided to play hide-and-seek with a twist—the seeker had to keep his or her eyes covered with a handkerchief while seeking. The children found a handkerchief and decided that Meenu would be the first to seek.

Meenu rebelled, 'I don't want to be the first one.'

'Come on, everyone will have to do it. Start, Meenu!' they all started to clamour.

Reluctantly, she agreed. Everyone ran away from her at first and she wasn't able to seek anyone. After some time, Anoushka felt sorry for her and touched her just so that it would be her turn, and Meenu would be free.

Now Anoushka had to blind herself. She found it hard to catch anyone too. Soon, she pretended to be super tired and stood quietly in a corner. Soon enough, Aditi tripped on her foot and was caught. When it was Aditi's turn, she caught Raghu immediately!

Meenu sighed, 'I am short. Besides, I find it hard to run fast. I was afraid to go first because I really felt that I could never seek anyone and would have to remain blind for the rest of the game!'

Aditi said, 'Let me tell you a secret—the handkerchief was not tied properly and I could easily see your shadows in front of my eyes. It was easy for me to catch Raghu.'

'Have you ever thought about how hard it is for someone who is born blind, or becomes visually challenged for any reason? We must thank God for whatever we have been blessed with—eyes to see, ears to hear, tongue to taste, legs to walk and a brain to think. Being at the right place at the right time can change our lives!' said Ajja.

'Yes,' added Ajji, 'like the two blind beggars.'

Once upon a time, there lived a blind beggar Ravi, who begged from door to door every day.

One day, he met another beggar Vivek, who was also blind like him. They decided to beg together.

Vivek would always take the better portion of the food that they received. Every day, he would take the soft portion of the bread and leave the crust for Ravi. Time passed, and Ravi grew tired of this.

One day, Vivek left Ravi near a forest after they had walked for miles. He said, 'Brother, I have some work in a village nearby. Rest here and I will be back soon.'

Ravi was feeling tired and sat down on a rock to wait for Vivek. Hours passed and there was no sign of Vivek. The day turned into night and Ravi realized that Vivek was never coming back. Hungry and with no place to go, Ravi decided to walk and see if he would run into someone who could help. Unfortunately, his path took him straight into the middle of a thick forest.

After he had entered the forest, he realized through his senses where he was. It was the middle of the night. Suddenly, Ravi heard some footsteps and managed to find a huge bush. He hid behind it.

The footsteps came closer. A fox, a wolf, a rhino and a lion gathered for a meeting.

The fox announced, 'I know a secret.'

The wolf said, 'So do I.'

The rhino added, 'Me too!'

'I am the king of the forest, but I don't know any secrets,' remarked the lion. 'But tell me. I order you to!'

The fox said, 'There is a river one hundred footsteps from here. Months ago, I had become blind in one eye. When I went to this river and had a bath, I got my vision back. That's the useful secret I know!'

'I know a different one,' said the wolf. 'The king's palace doesn't get any water. What the king's people don't know is that there is a big, round rock in the royal gardens. If you move the rock and dig underneath it, they will find a spring—that water is healthy and enough to take care of the needs of the palace and the capital city of the kingdom!'

'Listen to this one,' said the rhino. 'The king's wife is unwell. Doctors have tried their best, but nothing has helped her. The medicine for her disease lies below a stream near the king's palace. If she eats five leaves from the plant that grows near the oak tree next to the stream, she will be well again.'

'I will keep these in mind,' said the lion. 'These are safe with me.'

The fox suggested, 'Keep them for a time when we might need to share one to make our lives better in the forest.'

'Let us meet back here after two months,' said the lion, and the meeting ended.

Ravi, who had been listening to this conversation, wanted his eyesight back desperately. He came out from behind the bush and walked a hundred steps in one direction. There was nothing there. He walked back a hundred steps to his original location. He did this twice more before he heard the sound of water and found the river. Carefully, he entered the river and had a bath. He began to see a little bit. He bathed for a little longer and saw clearly again. He was very thankful to the animals and the gods.

Now that he could see, he went to the capital city and requested for an audience with the king. He said, 'Sire, please give me some time. I will help you get water for the city and also cure your wife.'

The king was hopeful and allowed him to do as he pleased.

The same day, Ravi went to the royal gardens, removed the big, round rock in one corner and kept digging until he found water. Soon, there was a beautiful spring in the gardens.

Next, he found the oak tree near the stream that was close to the king's palace. Under the oak tree, he found a medicinal plant. He gave five of its leaves to the queen, which she ate and became much better the next day.

The king, pleased with his service, gave him plenty of money and Ravi bought a mansion and lived happily in the capital.

Almost two months passed. One day, when Ravi was standing near the gate of his house, he saw a blind man wandering around the street. He took pity on the beggar and called him to his gate to give food. When he heard his voice, Ravi recognized him immediately — it was Vivek, his blind beggar friend. Ravi modulated his voice and said, 'Some time ago, I saw you with another blind man. Where is he?'

For a few seconds, Vivek thought that he was hearing a familiar voice, but since he wasn't sure, he ignored it and replied, 'Sir, he is dead.'

'How did he die?' asked Ravi, surprised at his reply.

'There was a stormy night and the floods must have come and taken him away. Later, someone from our village found his dead body,' said Vivek with sadness.

Ravi took pity on his friend. He was lucky to have received his sight back, but Vivek hadn't. Ravi disclosed the truth, 'I am Ravi, old friend. You were instrumental in changing my life, so I will not hold what you have said against you. You left me in the forest and that's when my transformation began.'

Truthfully, Ravi shared the whole story. 'I happened to be at the right place at the right time,' he said. He advised Vivek not to betray anyone again.

Vivek asked, 'Will you take me to the river? I can't imagine what it would be like to get my vision back.'

'Animals can be cruel. Somehow, I managed to escape. If I go there, I am sure they will smell me and realize that I am the one who heard all their secrets. But I will come with you till a certain point and show you the way to the tree. After that, you are on your own, I'm afraid.'

True to his word, Ravi walked with Vivek till a certain distance and then pointed him in the right direction. Vivek started walking quickly, but he was scared of the animals. By the time he reached the tree, it was night. Though the time of day didn't make a difference to him, it makes a difference to the animals. So he decided to wait behind a bush until the morning.

In the middle of the night, a fox, a wolf, a rhino and a lion gathered for a meeting. They seemed worried.

The fox said, 'It has been two months since we met. Since then, I heard someone has found the location of the healing river. Only I knew the secret. Who has disclosed this to the humans?'

The wolf and rhino agreed that their secrets had also been revealed.

The three animals turned to the lion, 'We all had secrets, and it was a collective benefit to keep the secrets of others. You are the only one who didn't have a secret to tell. You must be responsible for revealing them!'

The lion snapped, 'I am the king of the forest, not a cheater. A king will not betray his subjects' trust.'

'Then who else knew the secrets?' wondered the fox.

'Perhaps someone heard us talking,' said the wolf, smelling the air. He used all his senses and the animals found Vivek hiding behind a bush nearby. He was petrified when he saw the animals with their menacing glares. Too late, he realized he was at the wrong place at the wrong time.

'He's the one responsible for disclosing our secrets!' roared the lion with anger. The animals attacked Vivek and killed him.

An Apple for Nothing

In the evening, Ajji was sitting with the children and showing them how to use their hands to make shadow-like figures on the wall in dim light. Though she was an amateur, it was still delightful for the children to see. Ajji taught them how to make different animals and shapes too. She said, 'I learnt all this in my childhood. Those days, I had no electricity and very few books. So I had to find ways to entertain myself. These days, there are so many mediums and so many animated stories for the kids to see—it is considered art and a big field on its own. People often fantasized about magic when I was young. When a magician came to our village, all of us used to gather around him and watch him in amazement. It was much later that we realized that it was simply art and science, and that anyone could learn and excel in it.'

'Ajji, you barely told us any stories about magic. Come, please tell us one about magic,' said Krishna. 'I looooove magic!'

'And don't try to teach us anything through this! Please, Ajji,' pleaded Anoushka.

Once upon a time, there lived a farmer named Madhu. He was a good farmer but also a miser. He worked very hard and grew a lot of apples. He put them all in a cart and took them to the market to sell.

There was a poor old man sitting in the market square. He looked famished. He asked Madhu, 'O farmer! Will you give me one apple? I am very hungry.'

'No,' said Madhu.

'But I am starving and I haven't eaten in more than a day. You have so many apples in your cart. Will you not give me one?' asked the old man, unfazed.

'Of course not! I have worked really hard to nurture each one for sale. Go ask someone else.'

'Please, farmer!'

'Go away, old man!' snapped Madhu.

'Give me one apple and you will have my blessings.'

'I don't need your blessings, old man. I need money,' said Madhu harshly.

The old man smiled at him. He said, 'Everyone needs blessings, child.'

'Blessings will not bring me profit,' said Madhu and began to argue with him.

A kind, compassionate woman who was passing by bought one apple and gave it to the old man.

Before the old man started to eat, he made an announcement in the market square, 'I invite all of you to come here and eat as many apples as you want.'

People chuckled. What was the poor man talking about?

Madhu laughed at him. 'If you had anything to eat or give, you would not have begged me for an apple.'

'Wait. Let me eat.'

The old man finished the apple, took the seeds and planted them in a pit nearby and covered it with mud. He asked for water and someone from the market square gave him a pot of water. He poured it on the apple seeds.

Within a few seconds, a sapling appeared.

Within a few minutes, it became a tree.

Within a half-hour, red and tempting apples were hanging from the tree. By then, a big crowd had gathered around the man.

The old man announced, 'Come, eat the apples from the tree.'

People were pleasantly surprised to get a free apple. Many took one and went their ways while eating it. Madhu also took one apple from the tree and placed it in his pocket, wondering what he had just seen.

The old man cut the tree down with an axe and began to get ready to leave the market with the pieces of wood on his shoulder.

Madhu was frustrated. He thought, *Why should I work so hard for a cart of apples? This old man distributed more than a cart of apples to everyone in less than an hour. I must learn this trick from him so that I can also grow fruits and become rich quickly.*

He saw the old man leaving the market.

Madhu turned to his cart, asked the mango vendor standing next to him to look after his apples, and turned towards the direction of the old man. But there was no sign of the old man, the tree, its leaves or the axe.

Madhu wondered, *Did I see what I did? Was it really true or perhaps just my imagination?*

He went back to his cart—his apples had disappeared too! Madhu scratched his head. Absent-mindedly, he put his hand in one of his pockets. He found an apple—the one that he had taken from the old man's tree. He ate it—it tasted the same as the ones he had grown in his garden.

Oh no! The apples that had been distributed were his! The old man had created an illusion! It was magic! A great magician had cheated him.

I wish I had just given him one apple in the beginning when he had asked for it. Then I might have saved my entire cart. I have been penny wise and pound foolish, thought Madhu.

The Four Dolls

Soon, the news of the easing of the lockdown was announced. Flights, trains and buses had started moving again. Ajji felt relieved, but it was a bittersweet feeling. She was happy and sad—happy because life was going to inch back to normalcy over time and sad because Kamlu Ajji and the kids were leaving the next day.

The kids had been in their company for the last two months and had brought sunshine into their regimented lives.

'I wish the kids could stay here permanently,' Ajji said.

'It is always good to have cake,' said Ajja with a smile. 'But you can't eat it all the time now, can you?'

Sudha Murty

'I understand,' said Ajji, sighing. She thought of the country and the children's future and knew that it was better for them to return to their homes and schools. 'Life must go on,' she said. 'We have to be careful, and yet, continue our work.'

She wanted to send something back for the children. She looked at Kamlu Ajji, 'Damu is here. We are here. Let's make obbattu (a type of sweet chapati filled with jaggery, ghee, chana and other ingredients). Each family can carry a few packets, and we'll also send two big extra packets—one for Salma and one for George.'

'You make poha well, too,' said Kamlu Ajji.

'Then I will also make packets of those, and Meenu can take some extra for her friends in Mumbai.'

Ajja added, 'I like kodbale, the specialty of Karnataka. I am brilliant at eating but useless at making these snacks.'

Everyone laughed.

Damu offered his services. He said, 'Ajji, I will make it.'

Ajji said, 'Make several packets of it—you can make extra for yourself and Aditi's friends.'

Damu and the two grandmothers soon got busy making snacks and the day went by quickly.

The next day, Ajji got the children ready in the morning.

Ajji said, 'Remember the stories and lessons you have learnt in the last two months and don't forget them. Keep your word to your friends, be kind and help others. Keep your surroundings clean too! And please bring your friends with you next time.'

After an early lunch, Kamlu Ajji and the five children would set out to Bangalore with the office manager, who would come and then drive them back to Bangalore. From there, Raghu and Meenu would catch a flight to Mumbai.

'This was a very different holiday,' said Ajja.

The children hugged Ajja and Ajji and touched their feet. Ajji said, 'Study well! Compassion, wisdom, knowledge and courage—these four qualities will make you a good person. It is like a balanced meal— you must have roti, vegetable, dal and rice. You cannot eat only one.'

Ajji turned to Kamlu Ajji. 'We have spent more time than we have ever spent together and it has been fantastic! Without your help, I wouldn't have been able to take care of the children like this and we wouldn't have been able to share our joys and sorrows.'

'I came for four days and instead, spent the most wonderful sixty days of my life with you. I heard many stories, remembered some of my childhood stories and shared them with the children too. I will cherish this trip forever!' said Kamlu Ajji, as she held Ajji's hand tightly.

'We will all meet again,' said Ajja, 'but under better circumstances and not with the threat of the coronavirus looming over us.'

'Ajji,' said Anoushka. 'Please, tell us one story before we go!'

The children whooped and yelled in agreement.

Ajji grinned. 'Let me tell you one. It is about the blessing I just gave you.'

Once upon a time, there was a doll maker who was very good at his craft. He had a son named Anil.

When Anil grew up, he said to his father, 'I want to see the world. I want to venture out and find my own path. Please bless me.'

Unfortunately, the doll maker was not a rich man, but he blessed his son with all his heart. When Anil got ready to leave, his father said, 'I don't know much about the outside world as I haven't travelled much and I don't have any resources to give to you. I only have dolls. So take these four dolls with you. They might be useful to you in your journey. These are special dolls and I have crafted them carefully and dressed them with the best I have.'

Before Anil could say a word, the doll maker continued, 'The first doll, dressed like a king, carries wisdom.

'The second doll, dressed like a soldier, carries courage.

'The third doll, dressed like a simple man, carries knowledge.

'The fourth doll, dressed like a hermit, carries compassion.'

Anil didn't want to carry the dolls with him everywhere, but he couldn't refuse his father's wish, so he put them in his bag.

'My child, knowledge and courage must always work under wisdom and compassion. Only then will life be beautiful,' said the doll maker and bid his son goodbye.

Anil walked and walked until he reached a spot; it was already noon. He was tired and wanted to rest. He wondered out loud, 'Is it wise to rest here? Who can help me out?'

Suddenly, the doll that was dressed like a king, came to life. It emerged from the bag and said, 'It is important to have wisdom in unknown lands. The key to wisdom is observation. Look around before making a decision. Otherwise, people will take advantage of you.'

The doll went back into the bag.

Anil looked around him and noticed a snakeskin near a tree. He realized that a snake was around somewhere and decided to walk further to find another resting place. He continued his journey for some time.

By the time he found another spot, it had begun raining. He was about to rest when he remembered the king-doll's advice. He looked around and saw the footprints of a lion near him. *This is also not a safe place to stay*, he thought and walked further.

A few kilometres ahead, he stopped and looked around him again. He didn't observe anything of concern and rested there for a long time.

The next day, he decided to walk to the nearest city. When he reached the outskirts, he saw a big mansion with a lot of activity happening around it. He wondered, *How can I also become rich and own a mansion?*

The moment he thought so, the soldier of courage emerged from the bag and said, 'Have courage. If you don't, you will never be able to fulfil your dreams. A life without courage is never prosperous.'

'What should I do?' asked Anil.

'I don't have the knowledge to answer your question truthfully,' said the doll of courage and went back into the bag.

A minute later, the doll of knowledge emerged and said, 'This area looks prosperous because the land is good. Take a piece of land that doesn't belong to anyone.' Pointing to an area with boulders, the doll said, 'Take that. It has a gold mine. Be strong and courageous and begin work there.'

The doll of knowledge returned to the bag.

Anil went to the area that the doll had pointed to. He learnt that no one was using the land and found the owner's address after asking a few people. Anil went directly to the owner's house and bought the land for a cheap price. Within days, Anil began to rid the land of the boulders. Just as the doll had predicted, there was a gold mine underneath. Very quickly, Anil became one of the richest people in the area.

The doll of knowledge frequently came alive and advised Anil on how to expand his business and where to buy land. One day, the doll of knowledge pointed Anil to a land whose owner refused to sell it despite Anil offering him an increased market price.

A month passed. One day, the owner of the land — an old man — fell terribly ill and didn't have money for his treatment. With a heavy heart, he decided to sell the land. Anil acquired it and began building his mansion. He thought that he had fulfilled his dreams with courage and knowledge.

When the old man was handing over the land to Anil, his beautiful daughter Pushpa approached Anil with tears. She said, 'This is no less than cheating. You are rich and we are poor. Helpless people like us are forced to sell our ancestral land due to genuine reasons. I am horrified that we had to sell our land.'

Anil fell silent and Pushpa left with her father.

Though the girl had spoken harshly, Anil liked her. *I should marry a straightforward girl like her*, he thought and sent a marriage proposal to her.

The girl declined his proposal.

The doll of knowledge advised, 'Tell the girl that you will return the land to her father if she marries you.'

Still, Pushpa refused to marry him.

Anil became despondent. He was rich and had a big mansion and yet, the girl he liked was rejecting him.

Suddenly, he remembered the hermit doll. When he did, the doll came alive and looked at him questioningly.

Anil said, 'I have so much money and yet, I am unhappy. Tell me the reason.'

The hermit replied, 'You cannot win everyone with money. People will pretend to listen to you for the sake of it. The day the money is gone, nobody will talk to you. Instead, try compassion. If you genuinely care for people, then they will care for you too.'

Saying this, the hermit doll returned to the bag.

Next, Anil asked the doll of knowledge, 'What should I do to make people happy? How do I take care of their needs?'

'Build roads, ponds and hospitals for the poor. Look after the animals in shelters and care for the living more than you do for the money. That is the best way you can help people,' said the doll of knowledge.

Anil took the advice of both the dolls and started doing good work to address the needs of the people and the society. The poor had to walk less with better roads, they had easier access to water with the ponds he built and free medical treatment. It made them very happy.'

A few years went by.

One day, Pushpa came to his mansion with her father.

Anil was happy to see her, but he wondered about the reason for her visit. 'I'm sorry I took your land. You may take it back with the mansion if you wish. It doesn't matter to me any more, as long as you are the one who owns it.'

'No, we haven't come back to ask you for our property,' said the old man. 'I have received free treatment from the hospital you built and that is why Pushpa and I decided to come here. She has reconsidered the proposal seeing the work you have done for people like us. I have come to give my daughter's hand in marriage to you, if you still want to be with her.'

Anil felt ecstatic. He had failed to win Pushpa's heart with gold and money, but his good deeds had accomplished his desire anyway.

Soon, the two were wed and Anil invited Pushpa's and his father to come and stay with them. He thanked his father for giving him the right dolls at the right time.

Anil lived the rest of his happy life being rich, wise, courageous, knowledgeable and compassionate.

'What a story,' said Anoushka and heaved a huge sigh as she thought that it was the last story she would hear on this trip.

The Greatest Medicine of All

With their bags all packed, it was almost time for the kids and Kamlu Ajji to leave when Ajja's phone rang. It was from the office manager who they had been waiting for, to come pick them up and take them to Bangalore. He spoke from the other end of the line a bit apologetically, 'I am delayed as I am awaiting police clearance to travel to the village.'

Anoushka asked, 'Why does he need a police clearance? We didn't take it when we came here. Why do we need clearance to come to our grandparents' home? It has never happened before.'

Ajja pacified Anoushka, 'Child, things have changed. If people with infection travel, they will spread it. That is why there is a restriction on travel.

When you came, the spread of Covid was not as bad as it is now. Let us wait. Patience is a virtue often missing in your generation. You want everything as early as possible. You don't like to wait. Remember, waiting is also good at times. It is the first lesson of patience.'

'Oh, Ajji, will you tell us one last story while we wait?' pleaded Meenu.

'I think you all are always hungry for stories. I'll tell you one that I heard from my grandmother. A long time ago, there was a similar infection in 1918. It was called the Spanish flu or influenza. Those who were children at the time heard this story,' said Ajji.

'That must be your grandma!' yelled Raghu. 'And our great-great-grandma! I want to hear her story, Ajji!'

'That must be such a long time ago,' added Aditi.

Ajji nodded and began her story.

Veenu, a teenage boy, lived with his parents in a village. His father was the village doctor and his mother a housewife. They had a small house in the outskirts and had a beautiful herb garden. In those days, herbal medicines were very popular and often given to patients.

Veenu's mother grew herbs and took care of them as if they were her children.

Every morning, Veenu's father went to the village and helped the sick patients. He would come back home in the afternoon and first have a bath. Then he would eat lunch, rest and study in the evenings.

Abhay, Veenu's best friend, was the son of the village headman. Life was calm, peaceful and content.

One day, a stranger came to the village. He was short, thin and had unusual features. In the middle of the town, he made a loud announcement, 'I am a merchant and have brought my merchandise here. I am closing my shop in the city and want to sell all my wares before I go to my hometown. My prices are throwaway and I will be here for only two days. Please come and see what I am selling.'

He opened a temporary shop and people gathered around it. His wares were beautiful—teapots, silk, handmade fans, candles, mirrors, paintings and much more. The price, too, was low. These would be much more expensive in the city, and the villagers would have to pay for the travel too to get them. Besides, his wares looked more exquisite than the ones available in the city.

There was a heavy crowd around his store and Abhay and Veenu observed the store from a distance.

They saw the stranger coughing and sneezing. He often took out a handkerchief and used it. People, however, were too distracted by the wares and most did not notice that the man seemed unwell.

After some time, Abhay's father, the village headman, also arrived to see the stranger's shop. The merchant was hospitable and said, 'Sir, I need a place to stay and I am happy to pay for it.'

The headman replied, 'Please come and stay with us as my guest.'

The stranger agreed.

Veenu never had a chance to go to the store as he had to return home quickly. After reaching home, Veenu said to his father, 'The new merchant is sneezing and coughing often. He seems sick.'

Father smiled and said, 'It must be the change in the weather we are having these days.'

'But he uses his handkerchief and keeps it here and there in different places. People were touching the same wares that he sometimes kept his handkerchief on.'

'Aah, someone has become a doctor,' remarked Father and smiled.

'I don't think I should go near him even though his shop is beautiful,' said Veenu.

His father nodded.

The next day, Veenu went to the market and saw the merchant at a tea shop nearby. He was wearing a sweater and had wrapped a shawl around himself. He was talking to a man there. Veenu heard him say, 'I have been feeling feverish since I went to the headman's house. Maybe the room is very cold.'

His sneezing and coughing continued.

Veenu stayed away from him and went his way.

The next day, the merchant did not turn up. His temporary store was also closed.

When some villagers showed up at the closed store, the headman informed them, 'The merchant was a good man and had goods of excellent quality. He sold all his wares yesterday and left the village. I hope he will visit again.'

The villagers were disappointed at this news.

A few days passed. By now many of the villagers had begun showing similar symptoms: fever, cough and cold, especially the village elders. Some had fever, some were shivering and others complained that their bodies were aching all over. They all began visiting Veenu's father, the village doctor.

Veenu's father was a bit alarmed. 'Why is everyone falling sick?' he wondered. 'Normal flu does not spread so fast.'

Veenu's father gave his usual herbal remedies and continued his routine of having a bath after meeting his patients.

A week went by and the situation became worse. Many of the elderly in the village began to lose their lives. The young men and women also felt the effect of this strange malady and even difficulties in breathing.

Some were not able to explain what was happening to them. They said, 'I can't taste anything!'

Some said, 'I can't smell at all!'

Some were vomiting.

Fortunately, the children either had mild symptoms or no symptoms at all. The villagers came and pleaded with Veenu's father, 'Doctor Sahib, please help us! The remedies are not working at all!'

The doctor tried other herbs but nothing worked.

The headman also fell extremely sick and so did everyone in his house. The headman, too, visited Veenu's father now.

'This may be something contagious, so please stay away from each other,' said the doctor. He realized Veenu was probably right—the stranger's handkerchief probably touched many wares bought by the villagers.

Days passed and still, there was no improvement in anyone's health.

The headman said, 'I have decided to go to the city to get better treatment.'

Many other families decided to do the same. All the village shops were closed and the local school was also shut down. Parents kept their children inside the homes and the noisy playgrounds suddenly became silent. All that remained was the constant sound of coughing.

Nothing like this had never happened in the village before.

The doctor tried his best to help the villagers, but no one came to him any more. The villagers realized that his medicines were not effective. He felt left out and prayed to God to turn things around.

One evening, an old lady came to the village with a small bundle of clothes in her hands. She was tired. She searched for people in the village, but it seemed deserted. Exhausted, she sat under the village banyan tree.

Later, a few men heard sounds near the tree and went to see what it was. When they saw the lady, she shouted from a distance, 'I am just an old lady who has lost her way. I need shelter for a night and then I will head out in the morning. Will one of you please give me room for tonight?'

The men shook their heads and went back home.

The old lady was disappointed. She decided to walk further to the next village. She trudged to the outskirts of the city and reached Veenu's house. There, she stopped to ask for water. Veenu's mother gave her water.

The old lady said, 'Thank you. What is going on in the village? Nobody wanted to speak to me or even offer me a glass of water. I am a traveller and I only asked for a night's shelter.'

Veenu's mother replied, 'Please don't mind this. The people in the village are kind and would have taken you in under normal circumstances. They would have even sent someone to accompany you to your destination. But things have changed these days.'

She continued to speak and explained the situation to the old woman.

'Can I stay here for the night?' asked the old woman.

'Yes, but not inside the house, because of this unknown contagious disease. I will make all arrangements for you to sleep under the tree here and also give you food.'

'Thank you!' said the old woman and laughed. 'I thought I will have to walk the entire night! What a pleasant turn of events!'

Veenu's mother gave the old woman good food and the old lady stayed the night under the tree.

The next day, when she was about to leave, the doctor asked her, 'Sister, you must have seen such diseases before when you were young. What do you think? Will all of us perish?' He pointed to the stacks of books in his house, 'I have gone through many books, but I still don't have an answer.'

The old lady smiled and said, 'Yes, I have heard stories about such diseases from my grandmother. They say that a disease like this occurs every hundred years. There is no medicine that will work for this. Only the god of medicine can help.'

Veenu, who was standing at a distance, was enthusiastic to hear more about this and asked, 'Where does he or she reside?'

'It is a long journey, boy. One must travel through thick forests across the river and climb a mountain there. Behind the mountain, you will find the god of medicine. It is a difficult journey and perhaps even impossible. It must be completed within seven days. That is all that I have heard, though I have never seen anyone who has taken this path.'

'It doesn't matter. I will go,' said Veenu.

'Are you a fool? It is hearsay. You are a young boy. How can you travel such a long distance alone?' said his father, brushing his idea off.

The old lady said goodbye and left.

That entire night, Veenu could not sleep. He thought about the agony of people coughing, older people dying and children being left as orphans. 'Why can't I go and meet god? The worst that can happen is that I may not meet god, but I have to take that chance.'

The next day, Veenu said to his father and mother, 'Give me some dry fruits sufficient for a week. I am determined to travel and meet the god of medicine and return with a solution. Pray for my success.'

With a heavy heart, they agreed and wished him all the best. His mother had tears in her eyes.

'I will be back in two weeks,' assured Veenu and began his journey.

He crossed the river and went into the thick forest. It was difficult to cross the forest. Veenu chanted god's name and continued. 'If my intentions are good, please help me, Lord.'

That evening, he came across a young and beautiful girl crying under a tree. Surprised to see another human being in the dark forest, he asked her, 'Young lady, who are you? Why are you crying?'

'I am the angel of this forest. My father is unable to come and help me, and I must carry the wood home by myself. Today, I am unwell and unable to carry this heavy load.'

'I will help you,' said Veenu. He carried the bundle of wood and together, the duo travelled to a small palace.

After they had settled, the girl made soup for Veenu and said, 'You can rest here tonight. Father will arrive tomorrow.'

They talked and laughed for a long time.

Veenu slept like a log that night. In the morning, he said to the girl, 'Thank you for your hospitality. I need to continue my journey.'

'Stay here, please, my father will come soon. You were so helpful. Please meet my father. In fact, you can stay here forever.'

'My parents are in the village.'

'You can bring them to stay here too!' said the girl.

'No, I am sorry,' said Veenu. 'I have a duty to my people and I cannot live here forever. I must go!'

Despite repeated requests, Veenu did not agree to stay and left to continue his journey.

He travelled all day. Late that evening, when it looked like it was about to rain, he came to a valley and met an old man, who was walking slowly with a stick. Veenu asked, 'Grandfather! Do you need help?'

The old man laughed. 'What a nice change it is to have someone to help me! Hold my hand and guide me so that I can reach home as early as possible before it starts pouring.'

Veenu took the old man's hand and they walked together. By the time they reached a nice well-kept hut, it had begun raining. There was dal and rice in the oven and the old man shared the food with Veenu.

'Grandfather, why are you staying here alone?' asked Veenu.

'I am the god of the valley. My ancestors have lived here forever. Where are you going?' asked the old man.

Veenu explained his mission.

The old man said, 'You are a kind boy. If you stay here, I will make sure that the whole land becomes yours. You can marry anyone, bring your village people here and your parents too. The water here is like nectar and the air is so refreshing. There are no diseases here.'

Veenu refused, 'No, sir, I want to go back and help my people, and others too. Please, give me your blessing instead.'

The old man tried his best, but Veenu did not budge.

In the end, the old man gave in and Veenu left the next morning. He reached the mountain the old lady spoke of and climbed it. By the end of the day, he was at the top. There, he approached a tree, wanting to sit under it to rest.

To his surprise, he saw a couple resting on the other side of the tree. When they heard footsteps, they stood up. They asked him, 'No one has ever come here before. Who are you? Why are you here?'

'I am Veenu. I am here in search of a solution for a disease. But who are you?'

The man laughed. 'I hear many people are in search of many things. But I am glad you are here. I am the king of the mountain. This is not a mere mountain — there are gold nuggets and diamonds inside it. Come and have a meal with us.'

Rubies and stones lined both sides of the road, leading to a golden palace. Immediately, lunch was served. While they were eating, the king said, 'Look, I need someone like you — someone who is adventurous and young and helpful. You can stay here and be the future successor of the mountain. You can stay here for six months and you can spend the other six months of the year in your village.'

Veenu explained the details of why he had come and declined the offer.

The next morning, he woke up. He got up and didn't touch a single ruby or emerald or diamond pebble as he walked to the other side of the mountain.

He was quite disappointed with his journey so far.

A few hours later, he spotted a hut. He knocked at the door to ask for water. To his surprise, two men opened the door. They called him inside and offered him food.

Veenu was uncomfortable and declined the meal. His main aim was to gather the right medicine and go back. Four days had already gone by. He had to complete his task and return.

He shared his story with the two men and said, 'I am in search of a medicine that can cure everyone.'

The men laughed. It was a familiar sound.

One of the men said, 'There is no medicine, my boy. This is a case of humans destroying nature and creating problems for themselves. When they become greedy, such things happen. And it does happen once a century. The villagers were so greedy to buy the items that they didn't notice that the man was unwell. The merchant who came to the village is a destroyer who came in human form. When he was coughing and sneezing and touching things, people did not care about hygiene or him. They were immersed in increasing their material wealth. So the destroyer could easily spread the germs.'

The other added, 'People must keep their house and villages clean. Only then can the destroyer be stopped. If someone is sick, they must be kept in a separate area where there is ventilation. Provide them with healthy food and kindness in words to encourage positive thoughts. But hygiene must be followed. Hands should be washed often, bed sheets changed every day and baths should be taken twice a day. That is the only way to avoid spreading diseases to others. Hygiene is the greatest medicine of all.'

Together, they said, 'Go back to your village and practise this. Be kind to patients. If you do all these things and hurt them with words, the purpose is lost.'

Veenu listened carefully and nodded.

'When you both laughed, I could see the familiarity. Who are you both?'

'We are Ashwini Kumaras, the gods of medicine. We are the same ones who took the form of an old lady and came to your village. So when I laughed, it reminded you of her,' said one of the men. 'I am also the beautiful young girl in the forest.'

'I am the old man, or the king of the valley, and also the king of the mountain. We are pleased by your dedication to help others. Any normal human being would have accepted the offer to stay back,' said the other.

Veenu was happy he had learnt something that would help his people. He smiled and said, 'Sirs, I don't have much time. I must return quickly.'

'Don't worry, we will transport you back right now. But first, tell us, why did you take on such a journey?'

Veenu replied, 'I have been taught that a tree stands in the sun and gives shade to others. It also gives fruits to others, and shelter to birds and animals even though he's alone. I want to be like a tree.'

The loud honking from the car outside broke through everyone's thoughts.

The office manager had arrived.

'What a story,' said Raghu. 'That was beautiful, Ajji!'

The children agreed and crowded around their grandparents for one last group hug.

Kamlu Ajji held Ajji's hands tightly and said, 'I'll see you soon!'

Ajji nodded, unable to speak. She was going to miss her and the kids.

'Come on, children, it's time to go,' said Ajja and helped them load the bags in the car.

Within minutes, the car began to move. The children waved and said goodbye.

'They will see a whole different world now,' said Ajji.

'We are old and we must still be careful with our activities for some more time,' said Ajja.

Ajji nodded and Ajja patted her on the back, reassuring her that he was there for her even though the children had gone.

The two of them stood for some time watching the car until it reached the end of the road and disappeared from view. Then they turned around and slowly went back inside the house.